TYRELIA

BOOK TWO OF THE REALM TRILOGY

S R MANSSEN

Manssen Publishing House

All rights reserved; no part of this publication may be reproduced or transmitted by any means, electronic, mechanical, photocopying or otherwise, without the prior permission of the publisher.

Copyright © 2019 S R Manssen

First published in New Zealand in 2019 by

Manssen Publishing House

All characters in this publication are fictitious and any resemblance to real persons, living or dead, is purely coincidental.

ISBN 978-0-473-46850-7

Orders: www.srmanssen.com

For my husband, Craig

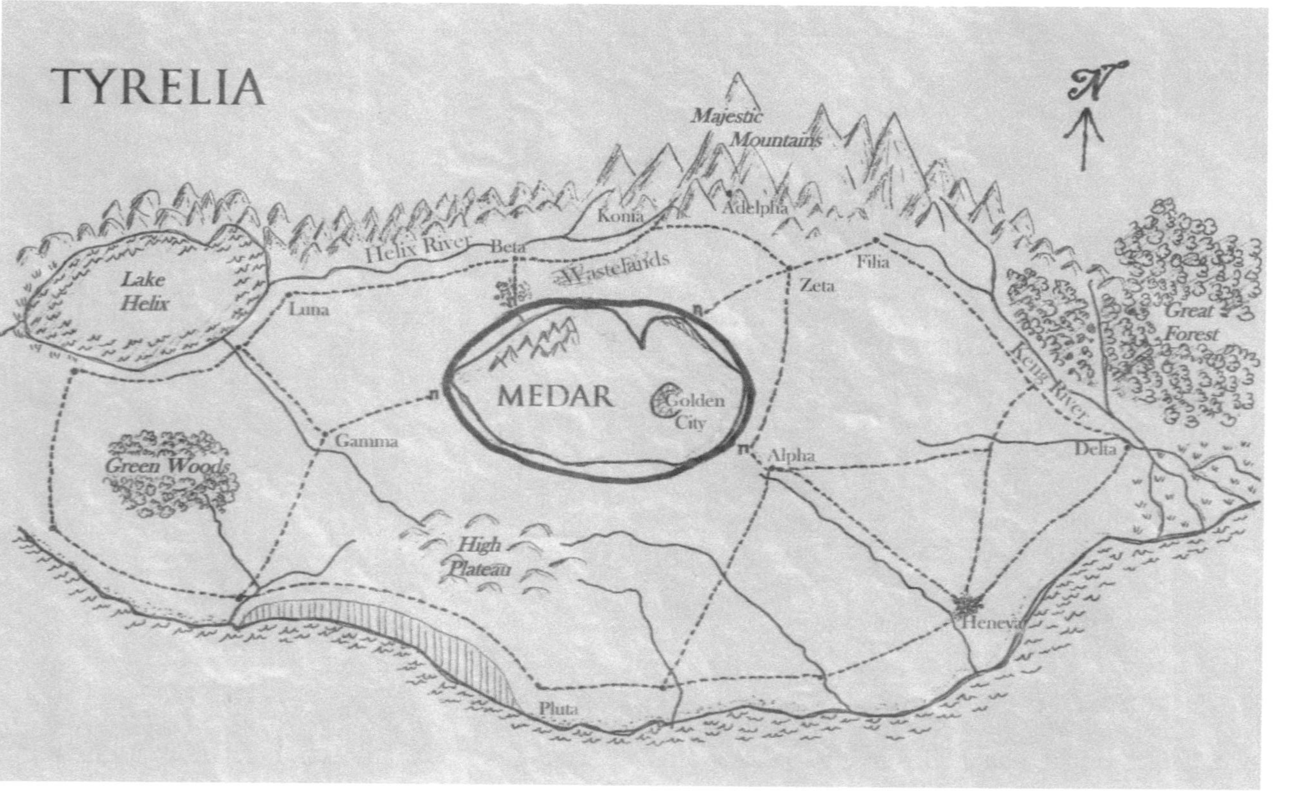

TYRELIA
N
Majestic Mountains
Konia
Adelpha
Helix River
Beta
Wastelands
Zeta
Filia
Lake Helix
Luna
MEDAR
Golden City
Great Forest
Keng River
Green Woods
Gamma
Alpha
Delta
High Plateau
Pluta
Heneva

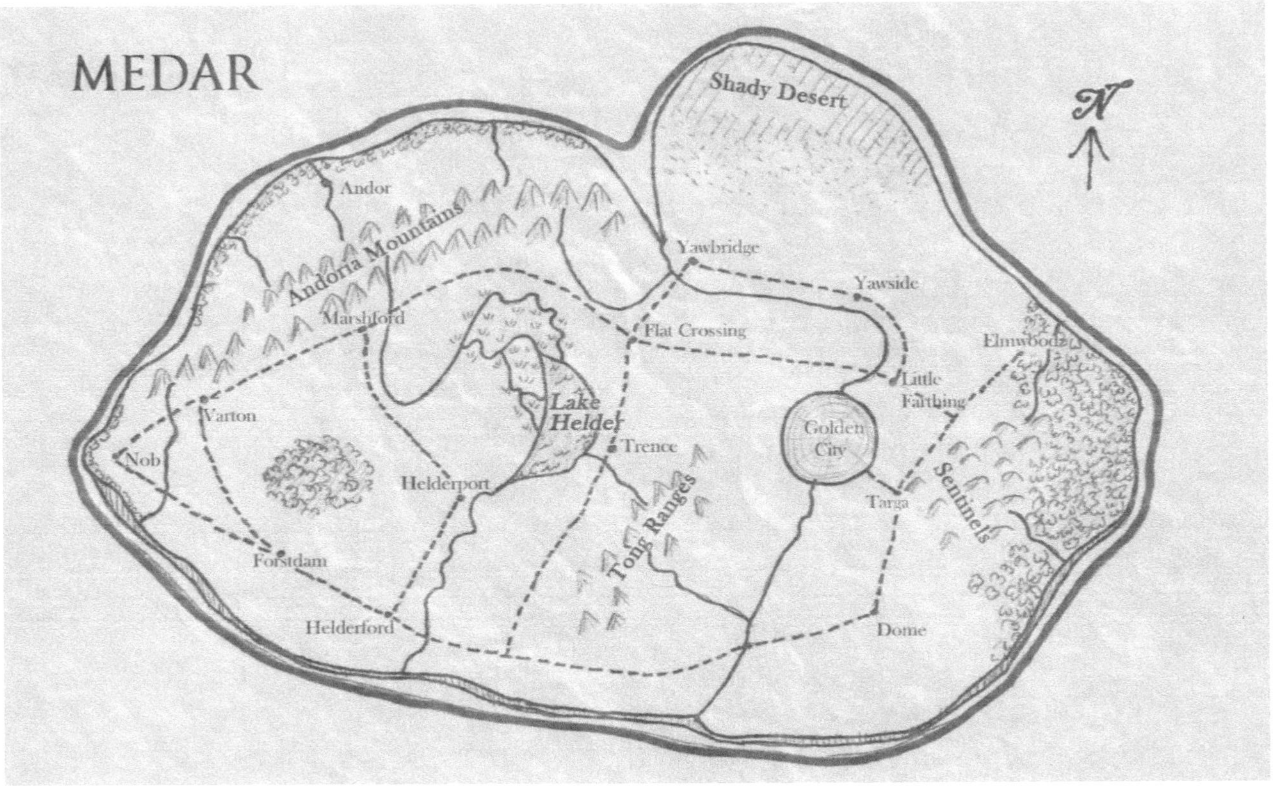

MEDAR
Shady Desert
Andor
Andora Mountains
Marshford
Varton
Nob
Forstdam
Helderford
Helderport
Lake Helder
Trence
Tong Ranges
Yawbridge
Yawside
Flat Crossing
Little Farthing
Golden City
Targa
Dome
Sentinels
Elmwoods
N

GOLDEN CITY

Level Seven - Acedia
Level Six - Gula
Level Five - Luxuria
Level Four - Ira
Level Three - Avaritia
Level Two - Superbia
Level One - Invidia

TABLE OF CONTENTS

TYRELIA

Tyrelia! Land of gold
A land so lovely to behold
O, land of beauty, land of light
Joyous refuge, pure delight

Tyrelia! That land so fair
Of meadows green and clean pure air
Of stately trees in forests vast
Of ancient rocks from ages past

Majestic mountains, white with snow
Their crystal tears to rivers flow
Splashing sparkles dance up high
Painting rainbows in the sky

Swathes of splendid floral hues
The land with colour do imbue
The golden sun smiles down from high
As he marches 'cross the sky

As flaming sunset turns to night
Stars and moon cast silver light
On all who choose to live lives free
From the Master's tyranny

He has no claim to any throne
He long ago was overthrown
By the Ancient, true and just
In whom all living things can trust

Who alone has claim to rule
Tyrelia, beyond the Wall
Tyrelia! O, land of gold
O, land so lovely to behold

Chapter 1

INTO TYRELIA

Freya took a deep breath and stepped through the Wall—the solid grey Wall that for her alone had disappeared. She turned back once more to look at her friends, the Watchers Saff and Thyst, whom she had farewelled just moments ago. They stood looking at the spot where, for them, Freya had disappeared. Yet Freya could see them clearly: Saff leaned against the Wall, his weathered blue robe wrapped around his tall, lean frame. Thyst stood with her back to the Chasm they had all climbed not even an hour earlier, her bow slung at her shoulder, over her purple cloak. Freya raised her hand, even though they couldn't see her.

Then she turned her back on them and Medar, to drink in the Tyrelian landscape spread before her like a feast. Never had she seen colours so vibrant—from the verdant green of the lush grass under her feet, the intense blue of the sky overhead, the deep purples and bright yellows of the tiny flowers dotting the meadow, to the deeper greens and browns of trees on the far side. She gazed at it all in wonder. A gentle breeze lifted tendrils of her honey-brown hair off her forehead, exposing her scarred visage with one blind eye, as she turned her attention to the thing that had led them to the secret bridge hidden deep in the Chasm: an archway.

It looked ancient. Roughly-hewn rocks stacked atop one another to form the rounded portal. Except, the stones weren't quite solid. It drew her like a magnet. She walked over to it and ran her hands over those closest to her. Rough, but not sharp. The points had been worn smooth, as if hundreds—no, thousands—of hands had done the same before her. The rocks were warm from the day's sun and were indeed translucent. She'd never seen anything like it.

She stood within the archway, her arms outstretched, her fingers brushing the rocks on either side, and glanced across the meadow. What was that? She screwed up her good eye in case she was mistaken. But no, it was definitely a path leading into the forest. And some sort of pillar adjacent to it. She scanned her surroundings, but the place was deserted. She set off towards the pillar.

And stopped. Something was behind her. She spun around … nobody was there. She shrugged her shoulders. Huh! It felt different. She looked behind her and gasped. She spun once more. The thing was on her back. She felt behind her. It was metallic and round. It protruded above her shoulders, which is why she'd seen it with her peripheral vision. With both hands she reached behind her. There were straps over her shoulders. Slipping her hands under the straps, she shrugged it off. She shook her head, bewildered.

It was a shield. The setting sun glinted off it. Its curved surface was covered with studs. She brushed her fingertips over them. It was beautiful. And completely strange. How had it got onto her back? Shaking her head again, she laid it on the ground and set off once more.

As she drew closer to the pillar, she noticed strange shadows on its surface. She broke into a jog. The shadows refined into markings then, finally, words. Panting, Freya reached out a hand to touch the monolith. It was stone. The letters were worn, indicating great age, but still legible. They read:

THE LAWS OF TYRELIA
1. Honour the Ancient
2. Put others first
3. Use your gifts for good
4. Follow the Rules

She stared at them for a while. Well, the first one made sense. The tablet that she'd discovered near her hometown of Nob in Medar had told her about the Ancient. She'd found it in a cave that she had practically fallen into whilst trying to escape from the village boys. The tablet was about the size of a small book and made of glass. When she shone a flame on its surface, words had magically appeared: a poem telling her about Tyrelia. It was only later, after she'd been torn from her family and almost killed by the Guards, she'd discovered that new words appeared in moonlight. It was then that she'd unlocked the secret of the tablet: the four numbers 50, 63, 92 and 99 etched into the bottom of its face turned out to be clues as to which substances would reveal further stanzas of the poem. It wasn't until she'd exposed the tablet to rainbow light that she'd learned of the Ancient. The fourth and final substance had been snow.

Her friends, Watchers Saff, Thyst and Rube—her father!— didn't think that the Ancient was still alive, but Freya had been convinced that he was, and now, there he was in the first law: Honour the Ancient. She smiled to herself.

The second law was nice. Put others first. That's just what friends should do for each other anyhow, she thought. But the third one: Use your gifts for good. What gifts? She didn't have any gifts—did she? What about the shield that had magically appeared on her back as she stepped through the archway? Had it been a gift?

Suddenly, she felt a weight on her shoulders. Her hand flew behind her head. She gasped. Sure enough, the shield had returned. She shrugged again, and its weight shifted on her back. Huh. Well, if the shield was a gift, what was she supposed to do with it? She had no idea.

Maybe 'gift' meant her tablet? Unconsciously, she rested her hand on the satchel at her hip, confirming the tablet was still there. She'd used it to find the long-lost path out of Medar and into Tyrelia. That was certainly good. Well, good for her. Except nobody else could pass through the Wall. She puzzled on that for a bit. Why couldn't the others get through? She tossed her head in exasperation. She just couldn't figure it out.

A thought popped into her head. Her talking stone! Maybe that was a gift, too? She'd received it from Watcher Merald, right before he'd died. He'd rescued her from the Pit that the Guards were going to throw her in, and just managed to tell her to find Watcher Saff. It hadn't been easy, but she had found him. It turned out that all the Watchers had a talking stone each—that's how they communicated with each other. She pulled it out of the pouch hanging around her neck and held it up to her good eye. It was the size of a quail egg, greenish in colour with marbled white veins running through it. They'd tested that the stones worked with Freya in Tyrelia and the Watchers on the other side of the Wall, still in Medar. In her final conversation with them, right before she'd passed through the Wall, they'd agreed to contact each other every night at dusk. She supposed that was also a good use of her gift.

She didn't have anything else that could possibly be considered a gift: she was still clothed in her leather tunic, leggings and travel cloak, with her satchel slung over the top. That was all she had. She was just an ordinary, nearly-fourteen-year-old girl.

Well, maybe not so ordinary, she thought ruefully. After all, it had turned out that she was the subject of a thousand-year-old prophecy and was the 'Daughter of Yaw'. Together with the Watchers, pursued by the Master's Guards, they'd followed the clues. Finally, just hours ago, they'd discovered the narrow bridge deep within the Chasm. But once they'd dragged themselves over the lip to the base of the Wall, only she, Freya, could pass through it. So, Watcher Rube—her real father (her heart skipped a beat again, thinking about *that* discovery)—had given her a new quest: to enter Tyrelia and see if she could discover the mystery of the Wall.

Freya turned her attention to the final law: Follow the Rules. Well, that seemed like a good idea. Depending on what the rules were, of course.

She glanced back across the meadow towards the archway. Rays of setting sun painted it a deep golden red. She squinted towards where Saff and Thyst had been. They were gone. Feeling suddenly very alone, she turned her back on the meadow and eyed up the path into the forest. The trees were not dense, and sunlight filtered through the leaves, dappling the forest floor. It looked safe. But twas it?

There was only one way to find out. Hitching the strange shield up on her shoulders, she stepped into the forest

.

Chapter 2

THE WATCHERS

Saff pushed himself upright from where he had been leaning against the Wall. "Well, she's gone then." He brushed down his dusty robes and adjusted his belt.

Thyst still stared at the spot where Freya had disappeared five minutes previously. She blinked and shook her head slightly, as if clearing it. "Yes, I suppose so. Now what?"

"I've been thinking about that. I don't think we should go back through Andor. Too dangerous — might be more Guards on the way."

"What do you suggest?"

"Not sure yet. But first we need to cross back over the Chasm before it gets dark, else we risk falling off that narrow bridge. Once we've climbed the stairs on the other side of the Chasm, we head towards the western end of the Andoria Mountains." Saff gestured across the Chasm.

Thyst turned to follow his gaze.

Saff continued, "We can follow the Andor river upstream — making sure we stay clear of Andor. I believe there's another mountain pass, which would lead us to Marshford on the other side."

"Sounds good. Let's go then." Thyst adjusted the bow slung on her shoulder and out of habit reached behind her to check how many arrows were still in her quiver. Only two. Too few. Frowning, she strode to the top of the stairs and started the descent.

The stairs were narrow and crumbling, a low wall the only thing preventing her and Saff from toppling into the Chasm. They needed both hands to balance themselves. Down, down, down they climbed. It grew darker and colder. They slowed, moving as much by feel as by sight.

Finally, they arrived at the landing at the base and stepped gratefully on to it, glad to be done with the stairs.

"Now for the bridge," Thyst whispered. Suddenly, an image leapt into her head of Watcher Paz crumpling in a heap and toppling off the bridge into the depths of the Chasm, clutching at the arrow in his chest. She sat down.

"What's wrong?" asked Saff.

"Nothing … just …" Tears welled up in her eyes and a sob escaped her.

"Oh. Of course." Saff crouched down beside her and placed his arm around her shoulders. He cleared his throat. "Paz was a good Watcher and a great friend. He did his duty well. But now his vigil is done."

"His vigil is done." Thyst echoed. She brushed at her eyes with the heel of her hand and sniffed. "Thank you, Saff."

He squeezed her shoulder one more time and stood up. "Ready now?" he queried, his blue eyes full of concern.

Thyst nodded and stood up. She eyed the bridge. It was extremely narrow. Without rails. Over an extremely deep Chasm. She took a deep breath and stepped onto it.

It was quite different from when they had crossed it only a few hours earlier. Then, they had been pursued by Guards shooting arrows at them. It had been intense, trying to help Freya across safely. Because the bridge was so narrow, they'd needed their arms for balance and had therefore been forced to allow Freya to be visible. Thyst had gone ahead of her, and an invisible Paz had had Freya's back. The arrow that had killed him had been intended for Freya. She sighed.

Now it was just her and Saff. She walked calmly and carefully, taking her time. Saff followed her, a few paces behind.

At the far side, the bodies of two Guards lay awkwardly on the platform where they had been slain, arrows protruding from their chests. Thyst strode over and wrenched the arrows out of them. Wiping the blood off the shafts with her cloak, she slid them back into her quiver. She looked around to see if there were any more. She spotted a third Guard on the second to bottom step and retrieved two more arrows out of him.

"Let's not leave them here." Saff said. Grunting, he dragged one, then the other, towards the edge, then pushed them off with his boot. Thyst dealt with the third Guard. That business done, they began the long climb back up to the top.

The sun was on the verge of setting by the time they wearily dragged themselves up the final step and fell panting amongst the dense foliage that grew right up to the edge of the Chasm on this side, concealing the stairway.

"I'd better call Freya." Saff exclaimed, eyeing the setting sun. He extricated his talking stone from a hidden pocket in his robes. It was blue, with white veins running through it. He placed it on his palm and focused his thoughts on Freya. A haze of blue formed around it. Swirling shades of blue solidified into Freya's face.

"Saff!" she exclaimed happily.

"How are you, Freya?"

"I'm good! But something very strange happened when I went through that archway. I've got a shield."

"What? You found a shield?"

"No, not found. It just sort of … appeared. On my back."

Saff scratched his beard with his free hand. "I don't know what to make of that, Freya."

Freya shook her head. "Me neither. And that's not all. There's a pillar with the Laws of Tyrelia on it. There are four of them: *Honour the Ancient, Put others first, Use your gifts for good* and *Follow the Rules.*" The words tumbled out.

Saff chuckled. "Sounds great. So, you're doing okay?"

"Yeah. How's Thyst?"

"She's good. We got back across the Chasm all right, and we've just finished climbing the stairs. We'd better move on now. Don't want to be found here."

"All right. Say goodnight to her from me. I'll call Rube now."

"You do that, Freya. Talk tomorrow."

"Bye."

Thyst mopped at her brow with her sleeve. "I'm really thirsty and my water skin is empty."

Saff stood up. "Mine too. Let's go find that stream."

They pushed their way through the dense shrubbery that grew all along this edge of the Chasm. Not only did the band of vegetation prevent people and livestock from accidentally wandering too close to the edge, but for a thousand years it had also served to hide the ancient stairway leading down to the bridge. Branches and leaves swished as they brushed against their bodies, snapping back into place behind them, leaving no trace of their passage. Eventually, they emerged into the paddocks and fields at the outskirts of Andor. They turned themselves invisible then walked along the edge of the shrubs until they reached the Andor River. Falling gratefully to their knees, they leant over the bank and scooped the cool water into their mouths.

Their thirst slaked, they filled their water skins. It was well and truly dusk now and, in the distance upstream, the lights of Andor town twinkled from the windows of numerous houses. Andor was built on an island in the middle of the river with multiple bridges to the shore on either side. On their journey to the long-lost path, only Saff had crossed the river by those bridges to lure the Guards into following him rather than Freya and the other two Watchers. The ploy had only partially worked, in that their pursuers had split their forces, and half had followed Saff, whilst the other half had followed Paz, Thyst and Freya.

Suddenly, they heard a noise.

"Shh," Saff hissed. He put his hand on Thyst's arm.

They peered into the gloom behind them. There it was again. A thumping sound. Like someone was stamping their feet. A shape moved. Then it whinnied.

"By the Land!" Thyst exclaimed. "It's your horse, Saff." She laughed with relief.

"Well, that's a stroke of luck." Saff reached out and grabbed his horse's reins, which were dangling from its bit. He patted it fondly as it nuzzled his neck. "I really thought I'd seen the last of him when I left him at the top of the stairs. He must've heard my voice and followed us here."

"It's a shame we can't find my horse, too," Thyst sighed. Paz and Thyst had left their horses on the opposite side of the river. Who knew where they'd be by now.

"Why don't we try, though?"

Thyst laughed.

"No, I'm serious. Jump up behind me. Thunder can cross the river."

"Okay. But you should try a bit further upstream. We were able to cross where there's a whole lot of little islands. They all lined up like stepping stones. It was amazing," Thyst recounted.

Saff found the spot and they crossed to the other side. Then he turned his mount to head back downstream towards the Chasm.

"We left them just in there." Thyst leaned forward from where she was seated behind Saff and pointed under his arm at the foliage. "Beside the river."

Saff urged his horse forward into the bushes.

"Dapple! Dapple!" Thyst called. She clicked her tongue. "Sandstorm?"

They strained their ears. Nothing.

By now it was dark. "You know what?" Saff asked. "I think we should just call it a night. We're well concealed here."

Thyst had to agree. There was not much point in wandering around in this vegetation in the dark. They knew that it grew right up to the edge of the Chasm, and they could easily fall in. She shuddered at the thought.

Saff hobbled his horse. They ate a light meal, then rolled themselves into their blankets and fell asleep straight away. It had been a long day. They had found the long-lost path to Tyrelia and crossed the Chasm. Twice. It was quite a feat!

Chapter 3

IN THE GOLDEN CITY

At the crack of dawn, an invisible Watcher Rube slipped back into the Golden City. He'd spent the night at the base of the city walls, trying to sleep, but the excitement of the previous day had kept him tossing and turning all night long.

The Golden City was the capital of Medar and home to the Master. It was a conical mountain surrounded entirely by a moat and a tall, gleaming white wall. The only way in was via the drawbridge to the single gateway. The dwellings within the city were perched one above the other on the steep hillside, like decorations on an elaborate cake. Narrow roads wound their way between them. All the houses were whitewashed, with terracotta tiled roofs, and many had pots of brightly coloured geraniums hanging from the windowsills. The Master's mansion, shrouded in cloud, crowned the city. It was said that it was covered in glittering gold.

The inhabitants of the Golden City were selected by a lottery system, and when Freya's family had been Selected, they'd considered themselves the luckiest people in Medar. Back in Nob, they'd led a meagre existence, scratching out a living in the poor soils in that part of the Land. Here, they were given a pretty, whitewashed cottage with glass windows and two bedrooms. They'd been assigned farming duties to work the fertile fields outside the city gates.

Freya's family had told Rube that before coming to the Golden City, they had thought that the reason nobody ever left it was because life was so much better there. But on the day of their admittance, they'd learnt otherwise. As they'd stepped into the entranceway, they'd been cast into gloom. As they blinked, trying to adjust their vision, hands had grabbed their arms and pushed back their sleeves. Something had stabbed their inner elbows, and a strange coolness flowed through their veins. An injection. At the time, the Guards had told them that the injection was not only their 'ticket into the Golden City' but also that it would prevent them ever leaving. As farmers, the family's injections allowed them to work the fields outside the city gates, but only to a certain distance. Any further ... and they would die.

Rube had first managed to enter the Golden City about a week back and, thanks to his ability to turn himself invisible, had escaped being given the injection. After spending nearly a week drifting invisibly through the city, two days ago he'd finally found Freya's family. That had been a stroke of luck: he'd been at the weekly Games, and 'Jack from Nob' had been announced as the winner of a wrestling match.

He'd followed them home and brought them up to speed with Freya's adventures—how he and his fellow Watchers had been able to turn her invisible, help her solve the clues that the tablet revealed, and figure out where the long-lost path to Tyrelia was. But, most importantly, based on Martha's description of Freya's natural mother, the woman from Yaw, he'd been able to confirm that she'd been his wife … and that Freya was his natural daughter!

However, it had not taken him long to discover that his talking stone didn't work within the city's walls. The day after discovering Freya's family, they'd helped him leave. He'd found a safe spot and waited most of the day, trying to contact the other Watchers. Finally, late yesterday afternoon, they'd connected. Freya and the Watchers had found the long-lost path, crossed the Chasm and were at the Wall. Except Freya could no longer see the Wall! They didn't know why or how, but Freya was the only one who could pass through and enter Tyrelia. And so, moments after finding his daughter, he had sent her off alone into Tyrelia on another adventure. But not before arranging with Freya and the Watchers to contact each other every evening at sunset.

Now, he crept back into the Golden City to update Freya's family on this latest development. Once through the gates, he headed up the wide boulevard to the right. He twisted this way and that, up a narrow staircase here and through an alley there, heading ever higher until he found the family's whitewashed cottage. He sneaked around to the back door and rapped three times, waited a few seconds, then rapped three more times.

Shortly, Thomas opened the back door, stepped outside and stretched, pretending to take in some fresh air. Rube slipped around behind him into the house. Thomas swung his arms vigorously, reached down and touched his toes, then stepped back inside, closing the door behind him.

Rube was now visible and stood resting his hand on the bench, his white hair a startling contrast to his smooth red cheeks.

"Have a seat, sir." Thomas gestured towards the kitchen table and four chairs in the middle of the room. "Martha, Jack! We have a guest."

Martha bustled into the kitchen. "Rube!" she exclaimed. "You made it safely back. What news of Freya?"

While she fussed around, fixing bowls of porridge with fresh cream and hot cups of tea for everyone, Rube recounted the previous evening's conversation.

"Freya and the Watchers found a secret staircase and bridge across the Chasm near the town of Andor." The family looked blank. "In the north of the Land, on the other side of the Andoria mountains," Rube explained. "And last evening, Freya managed to pass through the Wall into Tyrelia!"

He waited until the exclamations of surprise had ceased. "Unfortunately, the Watchers are unable to get through. We don't know why." He shook his head with frustration.

"So ..." Thomas said slowly, "Freya's all alone in Tyrelia?" He raised his eyebrows.

Martha's hands flew to her mouth as she gasped.

"I'm afraid so, sir." Rube replied. "It's the only way to discover what Tyrelia is all about. But so far so good. I've agreed with the other Watchers and Freya that we'll contact each other at sunset each night. But that does mean I can't stay in the city."

"What are you going to do?" Jack asked.

Rube sighed. "I'm not sure. I'd need to find somewhere safe to hide out, but also somewhere close enough so we can all talk each day—so I can pass on news of Freya to you all. And vice versa. Any ideas?"

It was quiet as they all thought for a bit.

Jack was the first to speak. "What about that big tree we all rest under during our breaks? Rube could hide out there and we should be able to somehow arrange to talk to each other?"

"Hmm, yes, I think that would work." Thomas mused. "Rube, you'd have to be up in the branches, I think, to totally avoid all accidental contact with the other workers. I'm sure one of us could lean up against the trunk. You should be able to whisper in our ear."

"Yes. I think the afternoon break would be the one to aim for. Then I could hitch a ride on a passing cart leaving the city for the day and find a safe place to contact the others by sunset."

Martha nodded and clapped her hands together. "That's settled then." She beamed around at them all. "Anyone for another cuppa?"

Chapter 4

DOUBT AND DESPAIR

Five days. Five whole days she'd been in Tyrelia, and still no people. She'd not seen a single soul. Just this forest going on and on. Tree after tree. The path she was following became narrower and narrower, until it all but disappeared. Tendrils of doubt snaked into her thoughts. What if nobody lived here anymore? Maybe *that* was why the Master had built the Wall—not to keep people out of Tyrelia, but to keep people safe in Medar. What if her being able to enter Tyrelia was all a big mistake?

After five days of trudging through this forest, her initial excitement had given way to doubt. Apart from a rickety old shack near the pillar, where she'd spent her first night, and on her second day discovering a moss-and-lichen-covered stone with the word 'Beta', an arrow underneath and the words '100 rata' etched into it, there had been no other signs of habitation. Maybe she was the only human in Tyrelia? A chill crept through her at the thought. The only thing that kept her loneliness at bay was her contact with the Watchers each evening via the talking stones.

Suddenly, Freya stopped in her tracks and turned slowly in a circle, scrutinising the ground, frowning. Where *was* the path? Her heart started pounding. Her eye darted from tree to tree. Which way had she come from? Her gaze settled on a large tree not too far away. Its thick branches grew low to the ground and were ideal for climbing. She slipped off her shield and satchel and set them at the base of the trunk. She reached overhead and, gripping a branch, placed one foot on the lowest bough and pulled herself into the foliage. Up, up, up she clambered, higher and higher, testing each branch before letting it take her weight. The higher she ascended, the thinner the branches. But she was not heavy. She kept climbing. Eventually, she emerged out of the forest canopy. She gasped, gazing about her, blinking in the sunlight.

A sea of leaves spread out below her in every direction: light green, dark green, yellow, brown and black greens, undulating with the varying tree heights. She shaded her eyes with her hand. No features to guide her in that direction. Freya manoeuvred around. She scanned the leafy ocean in the opposite direction. Oh! There was the edge of the forest. And what was that? She screwed up her good eye, peering intently. Yes, it was definitely a road. And cultivated fields! That meant people. That was where she wanted to go, then.

Not wanting to lose her bearings, Freya tried to keep facing the path she had spied as she climbed back down the tree. It was awkward, as the branches weren't aligned properly for it. She eased herself down, branch by branch. The lower she got, the further apart they were. A few boughs above the ground, she struggled to reach the next one. She squirmed her way along a branch on her belly, then gently swung her legs down. Slowly, carefully, she let herself slide down until her toes touched the branch below. She eased her weight onto it … but somehow, her foot slipped. Before she knew it, she was falling. She flailed her arms, ripping off a nail. She screamed. Twigs caught at her hair and scratched her face.

Thud! She landed heavily on the bottom branch, winding herself. She slid the rest of the way and slumped to the ground like a sack of potatoes. She lay there, unmoving. Then she moaned.

She opened her eye and stared up at the tree, taking shallow breaths. Breathing was painful. She lifted her arms. They seemed okay. Gingerly, she pushed herself to a sitting position. Ouch. She touched her sternum where it hurt most. Then froze. Her talking stone! Where was it? Frantically, she fumbled at the string around her neck and pulled out the pouch. She closed her eye in relief. It was still there. Wincing slightly, she pulled it over her head and worked her fingers inside to grab the stone. *No! No, no, no, no, no!* It couldn't be. A sob escaped her.

All that remained of her stone were crushed fragments.

Chapter 5

WOLVES

Saff and Thyst plodded gratefully into the outskirts of the forest, Thyst now mounted on Dapple with Sandstorm in tow. It had been a stroke of luck finding the two other horses the morning after finding Thunder. Since leaving Freya at the Wall five days ago, they had been travelling fast, putting as much distance as possible between themselves and Andor. Today they had ridden up and over the mountain pass, through the rocky, snow-clad terrain. Wind and cold had been their constant companions. It was a relief to finally have some form of shelter.

"At last, we should be able to find something for the horses to eat," Thyst murmured. "Not to mention me."

"Yes, let's follow this stream until we find a suitable clearing, then we'll make camp for the night. Keep your eyes peeled for berries and nuts."

"And some meat would be good too. I'd love a deer, but I'd settle for a rabbit."

Saff's stomach rumbled. He shook his head and rolled his eyes. "That is not helpful, Thyst."

Suddenly, a branch cracked over to their left. They froze, and instantly turned themselves invisible.

Thyst peered into the foliage, trying to see what or who had made the noise. Was it Guards? Then she saw it: a deer. She couldn't believe her eyes. Unslinging her bow, slowly, stealthily, she reached behind her and pulled an arrow out of her quiver. She nocked it and took aim.

Zing!

The arrow became visible the instant it left the bow, but it was too late for the deer. The arrow found its mark, and the animal sank gracefully to the ground.

Allowing themselves to become visible again, Thyst slipped from her horse. "Come on Saff, help me." She grabbed Thunder's harness while Saff dismounted.

"I suppose you want me to go and fetch it?" He raised his eyebrows at her, smiling.

"Yes, of course! That's why I brought you along," Thyst teased.

Saff retrieved the small deer. They trudged alongside the stream for ten minutes or so. The trees gradually grew denser and before long there was no trace of snow on the ground.

Saff stopped and threw the deer down. "Here's as good as anywhere," he announced.

Thyst handed Thunder's reins back to Saff then hobbled Dapple and Sandstorm.

Saff rummaged around in his saddle bags. "Aha," he announced, extracting his knife. He set to work skinning the deer.

Thyst gathered dry kindling and pine cones and before long had a fire burning. Saff cut some strips of meat off a haunch. They poked them on to the tips of sharpened green sticks and held them over the flames.

The aroma of roasting meat soon filled the air. Thyst licked her lips in anticipation. "Isn't it funny how I'd just said that a deer would be nice, and there one was. Lucky we spotted it when we did. Any later and it would've been too dark." She inspected her meat. It wasn't ready yet.

"Mmm," Saff replied. "I suppose. Speaking of which, we will need to call Freya soon. Eat up!" He delicately slid the strip of meat off his stick and blew on it, before biting into it. "Oh, yes. So good." He closed his eyes and tilted his head back, a smile playing on his lips.

Thyst grinned at him and did likewise. Mmm. It was delicious.

Saff stuffed a couple more strips into his mouth then licked his fingers. "I'd better call Freya," he said, eyeing the setting sun. He extricated his talking stone from a hidden pocket in his robes. He placed it on his palm and focused his thoughts on Freya. A haze of blue surrounded it, shifting and swirling, but did not solidify into Freya's face. They tried for a full minute.

Thyst wrinkled her brow. "Why isn't she answering?"

Saff shook his head. "I don't know. Maybe she's lost track of the time? Let's see if Rube's spoken to her."

Once more he concentrated on his stone. Before long, the blue haze formed into Rube's features. "Have you spoken to Freya?" Saff demanded without preamble.

"What? No, I haven't," Rube confessed. "Let me try, then I'll call you."

Thyst chewed a nail while they waited.

Saff sat staring at the stone, waiting for it to glow. There! He stared intently and held his breath. It was Rube. "And?"

Rube shook his head. "Couldn't reach her I'm afraid. Let's both keep trying. If either of us gets hold of her, call the other.

Otherwise, talk to you tomorrow evening."

Saff sighed. "Sure." He pushed himself to his feet. He found some rope and strung the deer up from a branch a short distance from their camp.

They would cut the rest of it up in the morning, take what they could with them, and leave the remainder for the beasts of the forest.

~

Something roused Thyst from her sleep. It was Saff, shaking her. "Wha..?"

"Shh," Saff cautioned. "There's something out there. And I don't think it's a deer this time."

Thyst sat up and peered around her into the darkness.

The horses whinnied nervously.

Thyst stood up and crept to the horses. "It's okay," she soothed, stroking them.

Suddenly, a deep growl issued from her left. A pair of yellow eyes glinted in the darkness, low to the ground. More growling sounded from behind.

Saff strode up and thrust a bundle at her. "Quick," he said in a low voice, "pack up your stuff. We're going to have to run for it."

"Is it … ?" Her voice trembled.

"Wolves? Yes."

Her fingers fumbled. She couldn't see what she was doing. She dropped her blanket on the ground. As she bent down to pick it up, a dark shape came flying at her. Sharp teeth bit into her calf.

Saff lunged, and, with a flash of steel and a yelp, the wolf lay on the ground, whimpering. Saff leapt onto his horse.

Thyst heaved herself up into her saddle, her leg an agony of fire, as a howl split the air and ten, twelve wolves advanced towards them from all sides.

"Ya!" Saff flicked his reins and dug his heels into Thunder's flanks. Thunder snorted and leapt forward, directly towards one of the wolves. It cowered as the black horse aimed a hoof at its head.

Thyst spurred Dapple forward hot on Saff's heels.

Behind them the pack erupted into howls and snarls.

Saff and Thyst galloped furiously for a few moments before Thyst dared to look back. The wolves weren't following. Why not?

Just then, a scream pierced the night air. A horse's scream. Sandstorm.

Chapter 6

WANTED POSTER

Hank slapped a poster down on the kitchen table. "Look," he exclaimed, "we've got another one!"

They had all finished work for the day and were at Hank and Leena's house, after young Sam had been sent to bring them there.

They crowded around the table and stared at the latest WANTED poster that Hank had printed.

"It's that same Saff fellow," Martha observed, "but now there's a ten-thousand-unit reward. My goodness, ten thousand units! What does that smaller writing say? I can't read it from this angle."

Jack obliged her. "For the murder of twenty Guards. Last seen in Andor." He whistled between his teeth. "Do you think he did it?"

"Didn't Rube say that Paz and Thyst killed some too?" Sam offered.

"Have you printed any other posters, Hank?" Thomas asked.

"No, I haven't."

"We'll check with Rube tomorrow, but they either don't

suspect the others, or don't have any evidence of them being there," Thomas surmised.

"We know Freya is safe in Tyrelia," Martha added. "Where are Saff and Thyst now?"

"Last night they were on the mountain pass heading towards Marshford. But like I said, Rube will be able to update us tomorrow."

~

The next day passed painfully slowly. It was the usual routine: wake at the first bell, collect their rations before the second, eat breakfast and then assemble at the gate by the third bell. There they joined a large group of farmers and, under the direction of several Guards, made their way to the fields outside the city gates. They split up into their separate work gangs. Today the men were hoeing weeds whilst the women harvested cabbages.

They always looked forward to their morning and lunch breaks, but their afternoon breaks were the most anticipated, due to their secret rendezvous with Rube.

When the time came, Jack raced to the big oak tree and threw himself down on the ground. Anyone would think he was simply exhausted. In reality, he was saving a spot for his parents.

Thomas strolled over to the tree and, stepping over his son sprawled on the ground, leaned up against the trunk.

"Thanks, son," he said gruffly, mopping his brow with his sleeve. He tilted his head back. "Are you there, Rube?" he whispered.

"Yes," came the whispered response from the branches above his head.

"Hank's printed another WANTED poster—it's of your friend Saff, but this time there's a ten-thousand-unit reward. It says he murdered twenty Guards. The poster also says he was last seen at Andor."

"Oh, no," Rube whispered back. "They are well clear of Andor. But even so, I'll warn them to be extra vigilant."

"Any news of Freya?" Martha asked.

"Umm … actually, we couldn't contact her last night. I'm sure she's all right," he reassured them hurriedly.

Just then, two more workers sat down nearby, chattering loudly.

Martha immediately bent down and pulled some hunks of salami and buns out of her basket. She handed them to Thomas and Jack. "Typical men," she grumbled loudly, "can't manage to fetch their own food." She sat down and leant against the tree trunk, biting into her bun.

Thomas and Jack slid down the trunk to sit next to her.

Shortly, the crack of a whip split the air. "Break's over!" a Guard yelled.

Jumping to their feet, they stuffed the last morsels into their mouths.

As they hurried back to the fields, Martha's basket, which she'd left at the base of the tree, simply vanished into thin air.

Chapter 7

A MESSAGE

On the morning of the sixth day since entering Tyrelia, Freya finally emerged from the trees. After the relative dimness of the forest, the brightness of the sunshine struck her anew. She screwed up her eye, shading it with her arm, waiting for it to adjust. A distance marker at the edge of the forest informed her that Beta was only 20 rata away. However far that was. She strained her eye to the horizon. The fields she had spied from her perch above the forest canopy were not as well-tended as they had appeared: weeds strangled the crops and there was no sign of people working them.

The fields reminded her of her own family's struggling farm back in Nob. Was she ever going to see her Ma, Da and brother Jack again? Even though she'd been separated from them for more than five weeks now, at least she'd known that they were alive and well from her conversations with Rube via the talking stones. Unbidden, tears welled up in her eyes. She brushed them away, then winced as pain stabbed through her bruised ribs. Yes, she'd lost her means of communicating with the only people she trusted in the whole world. Yes, she was sore. But her family and the Watchers were relying on her to find the Ancient.

She straightened her back and felt the familiar weight of the shield. That's right. She was also the subject of an ancient Prophecy. Only she could pass through the Wall. And for some reason, she had received a shield. Lifting her chin, she set off once more.

After a few hours, she stopped for a rest and a snack. She eased herself down on the grass beside the path and rummaged around in her satchel. Her food supplies were running low and she struggled to locate them. Frustrated, she grabbed the base of her satchel and tipped everything out. Her tablet spilled out of its leather wrapping, landing face down on the grass. Tsk-ing at her carelessness, she reached out and retrieved it. She turned it over and gasped. As she watched, writing appeared on the surface, faint at first, then clear and bright:

Tyrelia! Land of gold
A land so lovely to behold
O, land of beauty, land of light
Joyous refuge, pure delight

Tyrelia! That land so fair
Of meadows green and clean pure air
Of stately trees in forests vast
Of ancient rocks from ages past

They were the same verses that had first appeared when exposed to flamelight in the cave where she'd found the tablet buried. How strange that they should appear in sunlight! In Medar, she had often looked at the tablet in sunlight, yet had seen no words. Mind you, the sunlight there was so weak, compared with here in Tyrelia. Later, when she'd been running for her life in the Sentinels, the hills to the south of Targa, she'd discovered that more verses appeared in moonlight. Her heart started beating a little faster. Would Tyrelian moonlight work too? She'd try it that night. With renewed determination, she set off again.

Two hours later, she came across the very first sign of recent human habitation since entering Tyrelia: ploughed fields. She picked up her pace. There! Some sheep. Then, as she crested the brow of a slight hill, she spied a farmhouse. She stopped in her tracks, suddenly feeling uncertain. What if the people there weren't friendly? She approached slowly, straining her ears. A voice! A woman's voice. Freya sidled up to a gnarled old apple tree that grew in the front yard.

"Frederick! Frederick! Lunchtime!"

A baritone rumble issued from deep within the dwelling.

Freya peeked around the tree trunk, trying to catch a glimpse of the owners of the voices. She couldn't quite see through the window. Returning to her original position, she rested her head against the trunk. A branch laden with apples dangled in front of her. Her mouth watered. It was days since she'd eaten properly.

She stared at the apple, transfixed. No! She shouldn't take it. But, unbidden, her hand stretched out and plucked the juicy fruit. She bit into it hungrily. Mmm, delicious. In fact, she'd never tasted one so good. Holding the apple between her teeth, she quickly grabbed as many as she could reach and stuffed them into her satchel. Then she slid down the trunk and finished eating.

Now that she'd finally found some people, she realised that she didn't want to confront them. Maybe she should find out a bit more first? Happy with her decision, she pushed herself upright. Straightening her tunic, she adjusted her satchel strap and shield, quickly picked another apple, and set off once more, munching it.

Before long, she came across another farmhouse. A dog barked. It ran out and leapt around her. Laughing, she rubbed its head, but kept on walking.

Eventually, at around midday, she entered the outskirts of a town. Eagerly, she looked around. Brightly painted wooden houses each had their own lawns surrounded by white picket fences or neatly manicured hedges. Two young girls were playing with dolls in their front yard. Their mother kept a watchful eye on them from a rocking chair on the porch whilst she mended clothes. She glanced up as Freya passed. Freya raised a hand in greeting, but the woman just stared at her, unsmiling. Freya let her hand drop.

A man sauntered up the road towards her. He was tall and lanky with dark hair curling on his collar. Freya looked at him with interest. There was something about him that was different. She couldn't put her finger on it. The man looked her up and down, his eyes flicked to the shield peeking over her shoulders, then he averted his eyes and quickened his pace. He swung his gate open and strode through into his house.

Up ahead, two women with baskets on their arms were headed in the same direction as Freya, towards the town's centre. Freya followed at a distance, wondering at the unfriendly reactions. Oh, of course. How could she have forgotten how people reacted to her deformity? The past month she'd spent with the Watchers had made her forget. The Watchers had not only accepted her, they'd admired her. They'd been watching out for her throughout the past one thousand years, after all. The

Prophecy not only talked about a 'Daughter of Yaw', but one that 'was not blind but cannot see'. That was exactly what her deformity was. Due to an accident when she was a baby, her left eye had been damaged: the iris had turned a milky green and the eyelid drooped, causing it to appear half shut. It had not taken long to realise that she had lost all sight from the eye. When her hair was long enough, she'd worn it to conceal the abnormal eye as best she could. Nonetheless, the deformity was still obvious and had been the cause of much teasing as a child.

The road curved up ahead. She soon saw why. There, sparkling in the sunlight, was a river. The road ran beside it, at the top of a grassy bank that gently sloped down to the water. It was busier now, with more people coming and going, carrying baskets and packages. A square opened at her left revealing a bustling market. Off to her right, a flight of wide steps led down to the water's edge.

Aromas and noises assailed her senses. Freya looked around curiously. There were all the usual things being sold or bartered: fruit, vegetables, roasted nuts, breads and sweet buns with raisins. On the other side of the square were the live animals — pigs, sheep, chickens, ducks — and eggs. In between were baskets, fabrics, pottery, shoes and other manufactured goods.

Trying not to draw attention to herself, Freya drifted towards the steps leading to the river and sat down. She studied the townsfolk from under her lashes. They did look different, the same sort of different that she'd noticed about that man. It was almost as if they were glowing. Or maybe it was just because the sun was so bright that it reflected off them somehow.

She inhaled deeply. All the tantalising smells made her stomach rumble. She didn't have any money to buy anything, but then she remembered the apples she'd stuffed into her satchel. Smiling in anticipation, she reached into her bag and felt around. Where were they? Frustrated, she pulled it to her front and flipped the flap open. In desperation, she shoved her hand around and, somehow, knocked her tablet out. It slid down the bank, leaving its leather wrapping behind as it did so.

Yelping, Freya leapt up and chased it. It came to a stop in the mud at the water's edge. Relieved, Freya picked it up. Mud smeared the surface. Crouching down, she dipped it into the clear waters and rubbed the offending muck off. She gasped. To her amazement, writing was again appearing on the surface, faint at first, then brighter. The words were different this time. They read:

Fresh clean air, sparkling waters
Quench your thirst, sons and daughters
Head to the place with sulphurous steam
To free Medar from the Master's schemes

Freya stared at them for a minute, her heart hammering. Then she started counting. She knew that the first two verses contained forty-five words, but the first number etched into the face of the tablet was '50'. She counted the words of these new verses starting at forty-six. The fiftieth word was 'waters' and the sixty-third 'steam'. These new verses brought the total word count to seventy. But she knew what she needed to do to unlock more verses: expose the tablet to sulphurous steam. The word 'waters' confirmed that words also obviously appeared with water.

Excitement built in her chest, but then she sighed. If only she could share her discovery with the others.

Chapter 8

WILLOW

"Hello, you're not from around here, are you?"

Startled, Freya jumped and looked around to see who had spoken. The person was seated a few steps behind her. A cap, the type farmers wore, hung low over a face concealed in shadow. Short blond hair touched the collar of the pale blue homespun shirt. Long legs were clad in rough, dark trousers and workers' boots. At a glance, this person might be mistaken for a man. But from the voice, Freya knew she was a girl.

"N—no," Freya stammered, wondering where to start and how much to say, if anything at all. "I'm not."

"Sorry, didn't mean to scare you. I'm Willow." The lanky girl held out her hand to Freya. "I'm not from around here either. Betans are such snobs, aren't they?"

Not wanting to be rude, Freya shook the proffered hand. "I'm Freya. Nice to meet you."

"I couldn't help notice you grabbing that thing that fell out of your satchel. So, it's all right then?" Willow inclined her head, glancing at Freya's hands.

Freya looked down at the tablet that was resting in her lap. It had dried, and the writing was fading. "Oh, this old thing? Yeah, it's fine. Fine." She turned away and stuffed it into her satchel.

"You know …" they both started at once.

"Sorry, you go first," Freya said.

"No, no, you go." Willow grinned.

"It's just … I'm really thirsty. Can you show me where a well is to fill my water skin?"

Willow looked at her curiously. "You really aren't from around here, are you?" she mused. She shrugged and stood up. She was very tall. "Come on. This way."

Willow led Freya back up the steps towards the market square. She wove her way between various stalls and people right to the middle of the square to a well. Above the well was a wooden frame with a bucket tied to it by a rope. A sign was nailed to the frame. It read:

Quench your thirst, sons and daughters

Freya gasped and came to a halt, staring at the sign.

"What's wrong?" Willow asked, stretching a hand out to Freya. "You've gone sort of pale."

"Oh, it's just … what does that sign mean?"

Willow glanced at it. "That? Oh, it's a Rule."

"That's a Rule? To drink water?"

"Sure." Willow laughed, shaking her head at Freya. "Here, let me draw some for you." She unwound the rope and let down the bucket with a splash. She pulled it back up and rested it on the side of the well.

Freya grabbed her water skin and dipped it into the bucket until it was full.

Then she drank. And drank. The cool liquid was like nothing

she'd ever tasted before. Yet it was just water. Freya brushed her mouth with her sleeve. "Aaah." She closed her eye and tipped her head back. "That was delicious. Thank you."

Willow laughed again. "Don't thank me. Thank the Ancient. His water." She shrugged her shoulders.

The Ancient's water. Willow believed in the Ancient. Freya decided to confide in Willow. She took a deep breath. "Umm, you've said a couple of times I'm not from around here. If I tell you where I'm from, will you promise not to laugh or run away?"

Willow rested both hands on Freya's shoulders and stared solemnly into her eye. "I promise."

"Can we go sit back down by the river?"

"Sure." Willow led the way.

They sat beside each other on the steps, close to the water's edge.

Freya turned to Willow. "I'm not from Tyrelia," she blurted. There, she'd said it.

Willow's hand flew to her mouth. She stared at Freya.

"Well, aren't you going to say anything?" Freya asked, clasping her hands together until her knuckles turned white.

Willow let her hand slip. "So ..." she said slowly, "you're from *there*? The Hole?"

Freya nodded. "We don't call it the Hole though. We call it Medar."

"How is that possible? We've always been told that everybody in there died a thousand years ago."

"Nope. We've been there the whole time. It's just that we've been trapped behind the Wall. The Master destroyed the bridge across the Chasm and somehow everyone in Medar forgot that Tyrelia had ever existed. Until now."

"So, what happened? How did you escape?"

Freya smiled, remembering. "I found a tablet that reveals messages. It told me about Tyrelia."

Willow glanced at Freya's satchel slung at her hip.

Freya flipped open the flap, pulled the tablet out and unwrapped it. She tilted the face towards Willow. Exposed to sunlight, words started to appear, faint at first, then brighter.

Willow's eyes widened and instinctively she reached for it.

Freya pulled it beyond Willow's grasp. "See the poem?" she asked.

Willow nodded. "That's amazing!" she breathed. "Is that what you rescued from the mud? No wonder you raced after it."

"Yes. And when I rinsed it in water, different words appeared. Look." Freya dipped it into the water at her feet and showed the dripping tablet to Willow. The words changed.

Willow read them aloud:

Fresh clean air, sparkling waters
Quench your thirst, sons and daughters
Head to the place with sulphurous steam
To free Medar from the Master's schemes

"I had just read *Quench your thirst, sons and daughters*," Freya explained, "and then I saw the same words on the sign at the well." She shivered. "Anyhow, in Medar, other words appeared when I exposed the tablet to different lights and substances. See those numbers at the bottom? They're a code. You count the words in the poem and, whichever word you land on, for each of those numbers, is another light or substance that will unlock more clues."

Willow looked confused.

"The first two verses that you saw in sunlight had forty-five words, but the first number etched into the face of the tablet is '50'." Freya pointed as she explained. "You keep counting the words of these new verses starting at forty-six. The fiftieth word is 'waters' and the sixty-third is 'steam'. That means that exposing the tablet to 'waters' and 'steam' will reveal more verses."

"Oh, I get it." Willow said. "That's why different words appeared when you submersed it in water."

"That's right," Freya confirmed. "And the next substance I need to find is steam. Sulphurous steam at that. Do you know where I could find some?"

Willow's face lit up. "Yes! I do. In the Wastelands. Horrible place, smelly and treacherous—it's about a week's travel from here."

"Oh." Freya's face fell. "I don't suppose you've got a map?"

"Don't need a map," Willow announced, clapping Freya on the shoulder. "You've got me!"

"Really?" Freya asked. "Are you sure? I mean, that's a long time to be away from your family."

Willow laughed. "My family doesn't live in Beta. I was just here for the market—been selling sheep, can't you smell?" She sniffed dramatically at her armpit.

Freya giggled.

"I was going to start heading back to Konia tomorrow morning anyhow. It wouldn't be much of a detour to take you via the Wastelands."

Freya smiled. It felt like a weight had been lifted off her shoulders. "I'd really appreciate that."

Willow grinned back at her. "It's settled then. Now, are you hungry? Let's find something to eat."

"Oh, I've got some apples. I was looking for them when I knocked the tablet out. They are the most delicious apples you've ever tasted." Freya rummaged around in her satchel once more, but carefully this time. She handed an apple to Willow.

Willow took it and bit into it. "It's good," she said between mouthfuls, "but nothing special. I'm not surprised they're better than what's available in the Hole, though."

Freya took a deep breath, about to defend Medar, but stopped. Willow was right. "Now that I think about it, everything I've eaten here has been really delicious. Is all food in Tyrelia that good?"

Willow wrinkled her brow. "Yep," she said finally. "I can't think of anything that's not."

"And," Freya said slowly, "whenever I was hungry, I always found food. Nuts and berries and stuff. Is that a Tyrelian thing too?"

"Yes," Willow agreed. "The Land provides. The Ancient makes sure of that." She said it with such conviction.

Freya frowned. "How do you mean?"

"Well, when food is plentiful—like here, in Beta—you trade what you need each day, using tokens." Willow dug around in her pocket and pulled out a shiny coin. She gave it to Freya to inspect. "But when you're out in the middle of nowhere, with nobody to trade with … well, you'll find food. Like the apple tree that you found, when you were hungry."

"Wow!" So the apples weren't stolen after all. Freya marvelled anew at how amazing Tyrelia was, and how wonderful of the Ancient to not let anyone go hungry.

Chapter 9

GAMES DAY

Saturday was Jack's favourite day of the week. Saturdays were Games Day.

The very first Games they'd gone to, they'd spent the day checking out all the competitions and activities: there were games of strength and endurance, such as wrestling, running, javelin throwing, and weightlifting. There were also competitions of skill and daring: tightrope walking, fencing, horsemanship, and archery. Although women were permitted to enter these competitions, it was not common; for any woman of beauty, it was far simpler to enter the beauty contest. They'd learnt that by entering the competitions, one could win gold. And with that gold, you could buy your way up to the next Level in the city. However, they'd also learnt that there was another means of earning money, and that was by betting on the competitions.

In addition, there was also dancing, drinking, card games and such. All in all, a fantastic day that everyone looked forward to all week.

Even before attending those first Games, Jack had dreamt of

buying his way up the city. His parents didn't share his dream, but then they had been rather preoccupied with finding out about Freya. He'd decided that his best chances were with the wrestling competition. At the second Games, Jack had been lucky enough to bump into Orn, a wrestling trainer. He'd begun training the very next day and loved it. There were a great bunch of lads also training with Orn. He'd quickly become friends with the brothers Straw and Hay. Those weren't their real names, but that's what everyone called them because of their hair. It was white blond, dead straight and, even though they kept it shoulder-length, it stuck up all over their heads so that it looked like they were wearing miniature haystacks. They were both burly chaps with biceps like melons. It turned out they were apprentice blacksmiths, and shared Jack's dream of buying their way up to Level Two and beyond. It hadn't taken long for them to become fast friends.

Jack was a quick learner and had been thrilled when Orn had deemed him ready to fight in the next games. He hadn't been so thrilled when he lost at his first competition match but, after all, what was he to expect? It had been his first attempt.

He'd worked hard during the following week at the nightly training sessions and had been rewarded by a win at the next Games. That had been just as well, because that was how Rube had been able to track them all down. Winning was wonderful, but he'd had to use his winnings to pay Orn for the training sessions. He was still a long way from being able to buy his way up to Level Two. Ten thousand units was going to take a long time to earn, when he only won five hundred units a match.

But today would be another chance to win a match and some money.

"Come on! Let's go already," he called.

"Coming!" His mother's muffled voice came from the bedroom. "Just tidying my hair."

Jack's father, Thomas, came into the kitchen and peeked into the basket sitting on the kitchen table. He helped himself to a piece of cheese.

"Why does she need to tidy her hair when she's only going to be serving drinks to those Guards?" Jack asked, exasperated.

Martha and their neighbour, Leena, had managed to obtain all sorts of useful information by overhearing conversations between the Guards whilst serving ale to them during the weekly Games. Between those conversations and the posters that Leena's husband, Hank, printed, they'd been able to piece together bits of Freya's adventures since they'd been separated and trapped in the Golden City.

Thomas glared at his son. "Don't disrespect your mother," he growled.

"Sorry."

Shortly, Martha came bustling into the kitchen. She saw Thomas's hand in the basket and slapped it smartly. "Don't you go eating all our lunch now," she reprimanded him.

Moments later, they were on their way, together with their neighbours and friends, Hank, Leena and their eight-year-old son, Sam. They joined the swelling throng making their way towards the Level One games arena. Close to the gates a crowd had formed, due to the constriction of the by-now familiar archways, which only allowed one person to pass through each time, and somehow caused the blood to throb in their veins.

Jack hardly glanced at the stern-looking Guards posted between each archway holding long, pointed spears. He was anxious to get to the wrestling ring.

Their pace slowed to a trickle as they were jostled and

squashed prior to passing through the gates. But once they popped out the other side like corks into the vast, circular arena, the crowds dispersed as everyone went their separate ways.

Jack and his family headed towards the seats stacked row upon row closest to the wrestling ring, one of the many fenced enclosures within the arena.

Securing the basket under their seats, Martha hugged her tall son and kissed him on the cheek. "Good luck, Jack. I'm sorry I can't stay to watch …"

"That's okay, Ma."

She smiled fondly at him and squeezed his arm. She then kissed Thomas on the cheek. "Leave some food for us," she warned, wagging her finger at her husband, before tucking her arm into Leena's and heading off to the Guards' ale tent.

Jack loped over to the ring. Orn had just arrived.

"Morning, Jack!" he barked. "You going to win again for me today?" He grinned, slapping Jack on the back.

"Morning, Orn. I sure hope so."

The other lads who would be fighting that day had also arrived.

"Right," Orn said. "Let's start warming up."

~

Half an hour later, a bell sounded. An announcement rang out around the arena. "The Games are open!"

The first matches in the lightweight class were between new and un-crowned wrestlers—that is, ones who had yet to win a round. There was Finn, the curly-haired opponent who'd beaten Jack in his first match of the Games, but who'd subsequently been beaten by Tom. Then there was the tall but scrawny red-haired lad, whom Jack mentally referred to as Carrot-top. Jack had faced and beaten him the previous week. The third competitor, a fellow with mousy-brown hair and freckles all over his face and arms, had also been there last week, but had lost every match.

Jack watched with interest. Either Carrot-top or Finn would win the round. He decided it would be Finn. Sure enough, he picked correctly. Jack wished he had money already so he could've placed a bet.

Then it was Jack's round. His heart started beating faster with anticipation. His first opponent was Tom, the chap with the tattoo on his bicep who'd beaten him previously. The fact that he was still in this round meant that he'd been beaten last week. That gave Jack hope. They stood facing each other in the neutral position, glaring, trying to intimidate each other. The referee blew his whistle. Jack and Tom lunged at each other. Tom grabbed Jack's waist and spun him, overbalancing him. Two points to Tom for a takedown.

The audience clapped.

They both fell, but Tom lost his grip and Jack managed to roll out from under him. One point for an escape.

"Go Jack!" his father yelled.

Before Tom had a chance to push himself up, Jack pounced on top of him, attempting to control him with a crab ride, but Tom flipped himself over. Jack was pinned underneath him on his back. No! He wrapped his arms around Tom and with desperate strength he rolled over. Now Tom was pinned under him. He'd managed to wedge his leg under one of Tom's so he couldn't roll back, but his shoulders weren't on the mat. One second, two seconds … two points to Jack for a reversal.

Thomas, Hank and Orn cheered.

Jack and Tom sprang to their feet and faced each other once more. They circled around for a few seconds holding each other's arms, before Jack hooked Tom's ankle with his heel and jerked it hard towards him. Tom lost his balance and fell heavily on to his back. Jack sprang on top of him and held down his shoulders, but he needn't have bothered. Tom was so winded he couldn't fight back. Jack had won!

Elated, Jack went over to Orn, who slapped him heartily on the back.

"Well done, Jack! Now, rest up. Here, drink this water." Orn pressed a cup to Jack's lips.

Jack grabbed it and took a big gulp.

"You'd better watch this next match. You'll be facing that long-haired lad next. His name is Smith."

Jack watched the bout between Smith and Tom intently. They were well-matched, and there was a lot of to-ing and fro-ing without any points. The referee must've decided they were stalling and gave Smith a warning.

Smith narrowed his eyes at the referee. Then he lowered his head and ran straight at the referee, bowling him over.

A collective gasp went up from the crowd. Some jumped up, booing.

Jack couldn't believe his eyes.

Orn and the other trainers sprang into the ring. One restrained Smith whilst the others helped the referee to his feet.

"That's it!" the referee roared, still panting heavily from being knocked over. "You're disqualified!"

A hubbub erupted, whilst Smith swore angrily and was manhandled away by his trainer and another man.

Tom stood in the ring. "So, what does that mean for the round?" he demanded.

"It means," the referee growled, "that the round is awarded to Jack. Jack beat you. You beat Smith. But because Smith is disqualified, the scheduled bout between Jack and Smith goes to Jack. Jack wins." He repeated.

Jack stared at Tom, stunned. Tom turned his back and stormed off to his trainer.

A man who'd been watching the bout ran up to Jack, waving a piece of paper in his hand. "Thank you! Thank you!" he crowed.

"What do you mean?" Jack asked, confused. "Why are you thanking me? What have I done?"

"What have you done?" the man repeated, chuckling. "Why, you've just won me a lot of money, you have!" The man poked Jack in his chest with his forefinger. "Thank. You." And he strode off towards the betting tent to redeem his winnings.

Jack watched his retreating back. Winnings! Of course. He'd won. Now there would be some winnings. He grinned and sought out his father with his eyes.

Thomas grinned back and gave him a big thumbs-up.

Chapter 10

A GHOST

It had been three days since the incident with the wolves. They'd been travelling the road towards Helderport and now, finally they'd made it to the outskirts of the town, located on the southern end of Lake Helder.

"We'll set up camp there," Saff pointed to a stand of trees. "That should provide us with shelter and cover for the horses, and it's still close to the lake."

"Right, but within walking distance to the town. We're getting low on supplies."

Saff eyed the position of the sun. "Still two hours until sunset, I reckon. That should be enough time to hide the horses, sneak into Helderport, grab some food and meet back here in time to call Freya."

"Oh, I hope we manage to contact her tonight. I'm so worried about her, Saff. That Ancient had better be watching over her."

Saff grunted and pressed his lips into a hard line.

They trotted into the coppice and tied their mounts to some saplings, not wanting to risk them wandering off while they were gone. Then, turning themselves invisible, they set off towards the town. After ten minutes, they came to a farmhouse.

"I'm going to go have a look around and see if there's anything we can take that won't be noticed," Thyst whispered.

"Okay, I'll keep going. I'll meet you back at the coppice in an hour."

Stepping off the road, Thyst skirted along the edge of a corn field, limping slightly on the leg that had been bitten by the wolf. She spied some cobs of corn growing on stalks just a few rows in. Pushing her way through the tall plants, she picked four of the cobs and stuffed them into her deep pockets. Next, she came across a field of potatoes. She knelt and dug up two large ones. She added them to the corn.

Finally, she came to a fence surrounding the farmyard. She studied the layout of the farmhouse and various buildings. She walked quietly to a barn at the rear of the farmhouse, giving the house itself a wide berth. The smell of animal dung assailed her nostrils. She eased the door open and slipped inside. It was dim, and it took a moment for her eyes to adjust.

Sure enough, there was a cow, a couple of goats and a big sow in various stalls within the barn. The animals shifted uneasily at the scent of the unfamiliar human. "Easy, easy," Thyst murmured, allowing herself to become visible and moving towards the cow. The animal lifted its head, hay hanging out of its mouth, and stared at her warily as she approached.

Thyst reached out a hand and rubbed the cow's nose, before moving alongside it, her hand resting on its back. Ah, that's what she was hoping for. She grabbed the bucket she'd spotted and pulled up the milking stool. Sitting down, she placed the bucket under the massive udder and pulled at the teats. After twenty squirts or so, she stopped. She looked around for a cup or mug. Nothing. Returning the stool back where she'd found it, she tipped the bucket to her lips and drank the warm liquid. Delicious.

"Thank you, cow," she murmured, patting its rump.

She slipped back out of the shed, invisible once more, and surveyed her surroundings. There it was: the chicken coop. She walked towards it, careful to avoid the mud so as not to leave any footprints. She went to the end with the nesting boxes and carefully opened one. Two eggs! She took one and tucked it into a different pocket in her robes. She opened another nesting box. There were three eggs in this one. Again, she took only one. She was just opening a third lid when a shrill scream cut through the air. Dropping the lid in fright, she spun around to see the farmer's wife standing staring at her—or rather, through her— at the nesting boxes, screaming. The farmer came bursting out of the back door and raced towards his distressed wife.

"What is it? What's wrong, Mary?"

Mary stood rooted to the spot, white as a sheet. She pointed a shaking finger at the chicken coop. "Th ... th ... there's a ghost," she stammered. "It's stealing our eggs."

Thyst took a step away from the boxes, careful not to make a sound.

The farmer looked in the direction his wife had indicated. "I don't think ghosts eat eggs," he said matter-of-factly.

"But I *saw* it, Dennis," she asserted.

Thyst took another step backwards.

The farmer lunged towards the chicken coop, flapping his arms. "Shoo, ghost, shoo!" he bellowed.

Thyst spun around and ran as fast as she could. The farmer's flailing hand missed her by a whisker. Pain shot through her leg, but she ignored it. She leapt over the fence, through the potato paddock, back past the field of corn and finally made it to the road. She ran back towards the coppice and didn't stop until she got there. Once amongst the safety of the trees she fell to her knees, gasping for breath. Her heart hammered in her chest and she shook uncontrollably.

After a few moments, her breathing slowed, and she rolled to rest against one of the trees. She took off her boot to inspect her wound. Fresh blood seeped through the bandage as another stab of pain shot through her leg. "By the Master," she muttered through gritted teeth. She ripped a strip off her shirt and rebound the wound tightly before easing her boot back on. She leaned her head against the trunk and closed her eyes. That had been too close for comfort.

~

Saff returned half-an-hour later to find Thyst dozing, propped up against the tree. He prodded her with his toe.

"Wake up, lazy-bones," he said, bemused. "Was it that tiring, pulling a few vegetables out of the ground?"

Thyst glared at him. "I got more than a few vegetables, thank you very much," she retorted, indignant. She fished into her deep pockets and pulled out the two large potatoes. She placed them on the ground beside her. Next, she produced the four cobs of corn and plonked them beside the potatoes.

"Look like vegetables to me," Saff remarked.

"And these!" Thyst announced triumphantly. She gently placed the two eggs next to the vegetables.

Saff raised an eyebrow. "Impressive," he said sarcastically.

"Well, I almost got caught collecting them," Thyst exclaimed. "You're lucky I didn't break them."

"All right, all right, no need to snap my head off," Saff placated her. "They'll go very well with what I managed to procure," he added. He fumbled in his robes and, with a flourish, produced a leg of smoked bacon and a loaf of bread. "How about that?"

"You did well," Thyst conceded.

"*We* did well," Saff corrected. "We'll have a feast tonight. But first," he paused to extract his talking stone, "we need to call Freya."

He placed the stone on the palm of his hand and concentrated on it. As it had done previously, the familiar blue haze swirled but, once again, Freya's image did not appear.

"That's four nights. Why isn't she answering? Maybe she's … oh, it doesn't bear thinking about." Thyst wrung her hands.

Meanwhile, Saff had called Rube. "What? A Wanted poster for me?" He shook his head, frowning. "Oh, no."

"At least you're well away from Andor where you were last spotted," Rube commented.

"Hmm. About that."

"What? Have you been seen?"

"Not exactly," Saff said quickly. "But … well, Thyst almost got caught stealing some eggs. A farmer's wife thought she saw a ghost."

"Oh dear. Someone might put two and two together: a ghost equals an invisible Watcher. You'd better leave there, fast."

"I know. And still no sign of Freya. Thyst and I are going to try and enter Tyrelia and find her."

"We are?" Thyst's mouth dropped open. "How?"

"Yes, how?" Rube demanded. "You can't go back to the bridge near Andor."

"No, we can't. So we're going to have to try another way."

Rube nodded slowly.

"We're going to have to find the Cave People," Saff confirmed.

Chapter 11

DIFFERENT

Freya woke refreshed. They'd stayed with Willow's aunt—her first sleep in a proper bed for weeks. They'd had a delicious breakfast of bacon and eggs, and now they were on the road again.

They headed due east towards Konia, keeping the Helix River at their left.

"Do you have more sheep to look after in Konia?" Freya asked Willow.

"Yes and no. I'll be going to help my brother look after our flock. But he's not in Konia. He's up the Helix valley, heading into the Majestic Mountains."

"Oh, you've got a brother? I've got a brother too. His name's Jack. He's seventeen. What's yours?"

"My brother's name is Alex and he's sixteen. He's my twin, actually."

"Really? You're a twin? That's so cool. I would love to be a twin. Is it great?"

"Yeah, it is. We get on really well. Finish each other's sentences. You may have noticed I'm a bit of a tomboy.

Sometimes we switch places. Once we went for a week before our parents noticed!"

Freya giggled. "Sounds like fun. My brother and I ... well, he's a lot older than me. We don't really hang out. *Didn't* hang out."

"Hey, what's wrong?" Willow asked, concerned.

"My family ... they're in the Golden City. That's the capital of Medar. We were all so happy when we found out we'd been Selected—one of the lucky few each year to gain free entry into the Golden City. It was supposed to be the start of a better life for us all. But then at the last minute, Grumpy old Garret told the Guards that I was adopted. I hadn't even known ..." Freya's voice trailed off.

Willow squeezed Freya's shoulders. "Oh kiddo. I'm so sorry. You poor thing."

After a moment's silence, Freya continued. "I wasn't allowed into the Golden City. But not only that, I was condemned to death. At the time, I thought it was because I wasn't a blood-relative, but I found out later it's because I'm actually a 'Daughter of Yaw'."

"A Daughter of Yaw? What's that?"

"There's a city in Medar called Yawbridge. It turns out that my real parents were from there. That makes me a Daughter of Yaw."

"Why would they try to kill you for being from there?"

Freya took a deep breath. "Well, because of the Prophecy— that a Daughter of Yaw would break down the Wall and free all of Medar from the Master's tyranny," she explained, shrugging.

Willow stopped dead in her tracks. She stared at Freya incredulously. "By the Ancient!" she exclaimed, turning to stare at Freya with admiration. "You're pretty special then."

"Yeah," Freya said sheepishly, "I suppose I am."

"Is that why you've got a shield? Because you're a warrior?"

Freya blushed as she reached back to feel it. "Oh no, I only got this shield after I entered Tyrelia. It just … appeared on my back."

"What? Why?"

Freya shrugged and shook her head. "I don't know. It's a mystery. One more thing to ask the Ancient."

Willow looked impressed. "You *are* special. Is that why you look different?"

Freya blushed again and touched her scarred face. "Oh, no. This was an accident. Most people have two normal eyes."

Willow looked confused. "I wasn't talking about your eye. I meant *you*. You look … solid. Dark."

"What do you mean?" It was Freya's turn to look confused.

Willow stretched out her arm and pulled back her sleeve. "Hold out your arm," she instructed.

Freya did as she was bidden and pushed her sleeve up. "Oh," she said, wonderingly. She could see it now. Next to her own, Willow's skin looked like there was light playing under the surface. There was a glow, a radiance about her. "Wow. I see what you mean. Is everyone in Tyrelia like that?"

Willow nodded. "It's the first thing I noticed about you. That's why I knew you weren't from around here. But I never dreamed you were from *there*."

They walked on for a bit, deep in thought.

After a while, Willow asked, "Did you say that you managed to break down the Wall to get into Tyrelia?"

Freya sighed. "No, I didn't. That's the strange part. The Wall … it just wasn't there for me any more. I don't know why. But it was still there for the others—my friends, the Watchers. You know, the ones I told you about."

Willow nodded.

"They couldn't pass through it. That's why I'm here alone. And that's why I need to find the Ancient, so I can ask him how to get the others through. And how to help my family leave the Golden City." She looked earnestly at Willow. "Do you know where I can find him—the Ancient?"

Willow stared at Freya with sympathy in her eyes. "I'm sorry, Freya, I don't. I mean, everyone knows he rules Tyrelia, but nobody knows where he lives or anything. It's not something I've ever thought about before—trying to find the Ancient," she admitted, shaking her head in apology.

"Oh." Freya was subdued. "I guess the only thing to do is to follow the clues in the tablet, then."

"Yes, I suppose."

They walked on. Freya took a swig of water. She still couldn't believe how good it tasted.

"Hey, look, Freya. A farmhouse. Are you hungry?" Willow asked.

"Now that you mention it, yes, I am."

Willow walked up to the front door with Freya just behind her and knocked.

They heard footsteps, then a woman opened the door. She smiled.

"Hello," Willow said cheerfully. "My friend and I were wondering whether you had some food you could spare for us?" She gestured behind her to Freya.

Freya smiled shyly and waved.

The woman looked past Willow at Freya. Her smile faded. She took a step back. "No, I don't." She slammed the door.

Willow stood for a moment staring at the closed door. Then,

taking a deep breath, she turned and smiled brightly at Freya. "Never mind, let's keep going."

"Do I really look that bad?" Freya asked.

"No, not bad. Just different." Willow strode off back to the road, muttering. "Stupid woman."

Within a few steps they came across a tree laden with oranges. "See," Willow exclaimed, "the Land provides. Let's eat."

They each picked an orange, peeled it and popped the juicy segments into their mouths. They grinned at each other.

"It's so good!" Freya said, closing her eye and tipping her face up to the sun in bliss. Juice dribbled down her chin. She wiped it off with her sleeve. She finished the orange and picked another one.

They set off once more. "So, tell me about the Hole ... I mean, Medar," Willow said.

Chapter 12

RENDEZVOUS

Rube sat in the tree, waiting for Thomas, Martha and Jack to arrive. So far, this arrangement was working well. Apart from Games Day yesterday, when of course nobody worked, they'd managed their rendezvous every day at afternoon tea time. Yes, it was working very nicely indeed.

Before long, he heard voices getting louder. Rube peered through the leaves. As usual, Jack was in the lead, eager to secure a spot at the base of the tree. Thomas was not far behind. Once under the leafy canopy, Jack flung himself on the ground at the base of the tree, whilst Thomas leaned nonchalantly against the trunk.

Thomas glanced about him, checking that nobody was looking. He rested his head back against the tree, and whispered, "Any news of Freya?"

"I'm afraid not. But we have a plan. Saff and Thyst are going to try and enter Tyrelia and find her."

"How? I thought they couldn't pass through the Wall. Besides, won't the Guards be looking for them?"

"They're going to try to find the other bridge, near the Cave

People that looked after Freya. The Guards won't know where they're going. Hopefully we'll figure out how to get through the Wall by the time they arrive."

Martha, who had come to stand beside her husband, handed Thomas a hunk of bread with cheese on it. He took it, then lifted his arm up and around his wife's shoulders. The bread and cheese disappeared from his hand during this manoeuvre.

"Thanks," Rube whispered. "Was there any talk amongst the Guards about that Wanted poster?"

Martha shook her head. "No. I suppose that's a good thing."

For the next few minutes they continued eating, murmuring quietly, to not attract any attention. They managed to sneak a few more portions to Rube.

A Guard approached them. "Right, you lot," he bawled, fingering his whip tucked at his hip. "Back to work."

"Yessir," they all chorused. One fellow was a little slow at getting up. Quicker than lightning, the Guard flicked the whip out.

The man yelped. A thin red line oozed on his arm.

Everyone hastily made their way back to their fields. Nobody else fancied being at the receiving end of that whip.

~

Jack couldn't stop thinking about the ten-thousand-unit reward. My, with that amount of money, he could buy his way up to Level Two. Still, it was pointless. Firstly, he would never tell anyone about Saff. After all, the Watchers had helped Freya. They were their friends. Secondly, even if he told a Guard right now that Saff was somewhere near Helderport ... he didn't know exactly where, and by the time they got there, not only would Saff and Thyst be gone, but because they were invisible, no one would have seen them anyhow. Pointless.

His thoughts turned to the man who'd bet on his fight yesterday. That was it. *There* was a way to make more money. He would place a bet. He grinned at the thought. He'd ask Straw and Hay at wrestling practice that night to show him how to do it. And then only six more days to wait until the next games.

Chapter 13

TONG

After their close call with the farmer's wife, Saff and Thyst had made haste towards Tong, only resting a few hours at a time before continuing. Now, on the morning of the fourth day since leaving Helderport, they had arrived at the Tong River. On the opposite bank lay the town of Tong.

They sat invisibly on their horses beside the road, eyeing up the bridge.

"I don't like it," Thyst whispered to Saff. "That bridge leads directly into the town. Somebody will be sure to hear our horses' hooves. It won't make a jot of difference being invisible."

"Yes, I agree. So, if we're not going to cross at this bridge, the question is, do we try to cross upstream or downstream of it?"

Thyst walked her horse over to the river. It flowed swiftly between two steep banks. It was too wide to jump their horses across, and too swift and dangerous to walk them across.

"I think our only choice is to try and cross upstream of the bridge," she whispered.

"Agreed." Saff clicked to his horse and they walked back to the road. Listening intently and deciding that nobody was around, they urged their mounts across the road and followed the river upstream.

The banks were still too steep and the river too swift for the next half hour. Eventually they came to a confluence with a tributary. "That'll be the Little Tong," Saff said in a low voice. "It flows out of the Tong Ranges."

"Well, that's a bother. We can't cross it here, so now we'll have to follow that one upstream. We're going in completely the wrong direction!" Thyst complained.

"There's nothing for it. Come on."

They set off once more. The river became narrower and narrower. After another half hour, Saff's voice floated out of the air ahead of Thyst, "We can cross now, Thyst."

"That's a relief." Thyst turned her mount's head and followed Saff, splashing across the stream. Then they turned downstream, back the way they had come, but now on the opposite bank.

Half an hour later saw them back at the confluence of the Little and Big Tong Rivers.

"Right, we need to follow the Big Tong upstream until we can find a suitable place to cross. But first, let's have a rest." Saff dismounted and led his horse under the canopy of an enormous weeping willow tree. Thyst followed suit. The wispy branches, drooping down until they brushed the ground, were bare this time of the year. They brushed their faces and draped across their shoulders as they entered the inner dome. In spring, the green leaves would turn this space into a hidden sanctuary, the willow's branches becoming a leafy curtain. But without the leaves, the bare branches offered little protection from prying eyes. They remained invisible.

Thyst walked over to the river's edge. The land had risen this side of the river, such that the steep banks were now a cliff. Thyst sucked in her breath. "Oh no, it's even worse now," she said in a low voice.

Saff came up beside her. She sensed that he was studying the lay of the land. "Yes, but look up there, about a kilometre upstream. Do you reckon that looks like a sort of path going down to the river?"

Thyst craned her neck. "Yes, I think you're right. The way the trees are growing on a diagonal down to the river—that's got to be a path."

They had a quick bite to eat and gulped down some water from their skins, then set off towards the path. In about ten minutes, they had arrived. Sure enough, a section of the cliff had slipped, forming a rough pathway down to the riverbed.

"I think we should dismount," Saff said in a low voice. "The ground's pretty soft underfoot."

They picked their way carefully down the slip. Loose rocks slid and clattered with each step, betraying their passage. But there was nothing for it. They had to keep going. Finally, they reached the riverbed and stopped at the bottom, looking around to see if anyone had heard them. All was quiet.

"Okay," Saff muttered. "Mount up again. Look downstream a bit, can you see that dip in the opposite bank? Aim for that."

Thyst nodded, even though she knew that Saff couldn't see her. She waited until she saw Thunder's splashes in the stream bed before she followed.

The opposite bank was much lower than the one they'd just come down. It only took a few minutes to cross the river and climb out onto the grassy slope on the opposite side.

"Nearly there," Saff commented. "Now we just need to follow the river back downstream and we'll come out at the other side of Tong."

They set off once more in single file, keeping the river at their right. They trudged on and on. It was close to midday by the time they arrived at the outskirts of Tong. They had wasted three hours with their detour, but at least they were safely across the river.

"Look," Saff whispered, "there's the road."

"What's all that dust?"

They both heard it at the same time. The familiar *tramp tramp tramp* of marching feet. Guards.

"Let's go check it out," Saff said. He clicked to his horse and trotted off towards the sound. Thyst followed.

Ten minutes later, they pulled up short. There in the distance, a long column of Guards was marching into Tong.

"I'm glad we didn't go into Tong," Thyst murmured.

"It's just a feeling I have," Saff observed, "but I don't think we should travel on the road anymore."

Thyst stifled a laugh. "Your sixth sense is amazing, Saff. So, what do you suggest?"

"Once these Guards are gone, I think we should stick to the river downstream almost to the Chasm. Then follow that around."

"Sounds like a plan."

It took half an hour before the column of Guards had completely gone. They waited until the dust had almost settled, before carefully picking their way across the road and into the scrubby grassland on the far side. As in other parts of the Land, dense bushes grew along the rim of the Chasm. They headed towards the line of darker green, trotting adjacent to the river. They travelled for a good hour before Saff called a halt.

"Lunch time, Thyst. There's nobody around. It's safe to be seen now."

They both became visible and slid off their horses. Thyst led Dapple over to the stream and let her drink.

"It's strange," Thyst said, I thought we'd be closer to the Chasm than we are."

"Why do you say that?" Saff asked. "We are quite close, I'd say."

"Well, then why can't I see the Wall already?"

"What do you mean?" Saff said incredulous. He pointed above the line of shrubs in the distance. "There it is. Are you blind?"

Thyst stared above the bushes to where the Wall should be. Then turned back slowly to stare at Saff. "By. The. Land. I can't see it. Saff, the Wall has gone!" She ran to Dapple, leapt onto her back and galloped towards the shrubbery. When she reached the line of vegetation, she slid off and pushed her way into the bushes. Saff followed.

Panting with exertion, Thyst shoved the stiff, leafy branches aside. They scratched her hands and face, before flicking back into place behind her.

"Thyst, Thyst, slow down!"

Thyst stopped. She was at the edge of the Chasm. She stared.

Saff burst through the bushes beside her, panting heavily. He looked curiously at Thyst. "Is it true? You can see Tyrelia?"

Thyst tore her gaze away from the breathtaking vision on the opposite side of the Chasm, of bright green rolling hills, a piercing blue sky with distant mauve hills on the horizon. She looked happily at Saff, a huge smile on her face. "Yes, Saff, yes! I can see Tyrelia. Oh Saff, it's as amazing as Freya said." She turned back to drink in the view.

"Oh," Saff said forlornly. "All I can see is the Wall."

Chapter 14

THE WHIPPING

Rube was incredulous. "You can no longer see the Wall, you say?"

Thyst nodded. "Yes. It's just like what happened with Freya. It's disappeared, and I can see Tyrelia. Why do you think that is?"

Rube rubbed his chin with his free hand. His other hand was holding his red talking stone, Thyst's head a swirling haze of various hues of red above his palm. "What's changed since leaving the Wall at Andor, and now?"

"Umm … Freya's gone?"

"No, not that. What's changed with *you*?"

Thyst looked away from her stone to Saff. "What's changed with me, Saff?"

Saff grinned. "You … stole some eggs?"

Thyst shook her head. "Actually … I guess with Freya telling us all about Tyrelia, it's become so much more real. I mean, I know as Watchers it's always been our task to watch out for the one who would fulfil the Prophecy and find the long-lost path to Tyrelia. But hearing all about the beauty, that pillar about the

Laws, the Ancient and the Rules and all that … Tyrelia is just so much more real. It's like I *really* believe in it now. Does that make sense?"

"Yes. But Saff and I have heard the same stories. Yet Saff can't see Tyrelia. I wonder why you're the only one that can no longer see the Wall?" Rube mused.

~

Rube had pondered on Thyst being able to see Tyrelia all last night and all day so far. Now, the seventh bell had already tolled, and he needed to be up the tree before the eighth bell tolled at two o'clock. That was when the farmers took their afternoon breaks—and when he would meet with Freya's family. He had some exciting developments to share with them today.

He had spent the night in a copse of trees off the side of the road, half-way between the Golden City and Targa. He was getting sick of sleeping out in the open, and the nights were cooling. He'd need to find somewhere more sheltered soon, with winter approaching. Still, the arrangement was working well. Every day, he'd managed to hitch an unseen ride on a passing wagon, both to and from the 'meeting tree', as he thought of it.

Today he'd clung on to the side of a wagon full of empty barrels. He'd leapt off with still a kilometre before the field with the tree. The wagon was going faster than others he'd caught, and he'd landed awkwardly, falling heavily onto his left hip. Now he was limping slightly. He was too old for these types of antics.

He limped slowly along the road at the edge of a field then, when he drew level with his destination, he turned and followed a furrow that took him directly to the tree, careful to disturb the soil as little as possible. There was nobody around but, even so, he scuffed his feet so as not to leave any footprints.

Within a few minutes he arrived. As he reached up to the lowest branch, a stab of pain shot through his leg. He yelped and fell to the ground. Rubbing his sore hip, he glanced around, seeing if anyone had heard him. Thankfully, no one had.

He got up and gingerly tested his weight on his left leg. He tried once again to swing himself up on to the lowest branch, but he couldn't manage it without being able to push off with both legs. He looked around him once more, wondering what to do. Oh no, the workers were on their way. Gratefully though, he saw that Jack, as usual, was leading the way. Rube pressed himself against the trunk of the tree.

As he had done previously, Jack flung himself on the ground at the base of the trunk. He landed on Rube's feet.

Rube couldn't help it. "Ouch!" he cried. Then added quickly in a whisper, bending down to Jack's ear, "It's me, lad. I've hurt my leg and can't climb the tree. Do you think you can stop people from accidentally touching me, please?"

Jack nodded and leapt to his feet. He leant against the tree, bracing himself with one arm, such that his body position prevented anyone else from leaning up against the tree trunk. "That okay?" he whispered.

"I think so."

Thomas arrived next. Jack quickly explained the situation in a low voice. Thomas promptly sat down at Jack's feet, in front of Rube. He put his hand on the ground, but instead it landed on Rube's foot. He quickly moved it.

Shortly, a burly man named Stefan stepped into the shade of the tree. He glared at Thomas and Jack. "There you are, hogging the best spots again," he complained loudly.

Thomas glanced up at his son. "First in, first served," he said nonchalantly.

"No," Stefan said loudly, bending down and grabbing Thomas's collar, "I think it's time someone else got to rest against that tree."

Jack stepped towards the man and shoved him off Thomas. "Don't you touch my father."

Stefan stumbled backwards. He straightened himself then, taking a deep breath, lunged towards Jack. He grabbed him around his waist, and they went sprawling on the ground.

"Stop it!" Thomas yelled, leaping to his feet.

Crack! A Guard had come to investigate the commotion. A black whip snaked out from his hand towards the two fighting men … but weirdly wrapped itself into a knot mid-air. Well, not really a knot. But it *was* wrapped around *something* in mid-air. Something invisible. Rube's arm. And then the unthinkable happened. Rube materialised.

The Guard stared in astonishment at the person who hadn't been there a second ago. Then, as quickly as he had become visible, Rube turned himself invisible again.

Thomas sized up the situation and ran to where he had seen Rube. He fumbled at the whip wrapped around Rube's invisible arm, trying to loosen it.

At that moment, Martha ran up. Seeing what had happened, she pulled a sweet bun out of her basket and offered it to the Guard. "Would you like a bun?" she asked brightly, stepping close to the Guard and waving it under his nose.

Confused, the Guard stared at her. "What?" he demanded.

Taking advantage of the moment of distraction, Thomas managed to unwrap the whip from Rubes arm. "Run!" he hissed.

Narrowly avoiding the two men still rolling on the ground,

Rube limped off in the opposite direction as fast as he could manage.

"Hey, you!" the Guard bellowed. He took off in the direction he thought Rube had run, flicking his whip out before him. But this time, the whip found only empty air. The Guard stopped running, panting slightly, and studied the ground around him, looking for signs of disturbance. He started down one furrow, then stopped, back-tracked, and started down another. After a minute, he gave up and stomped back to the tree.

Jack and Stefan had stopped fighting. Indeed, everyone was rather subdued, and stood around under the tree.

"Just wait until I get to the bottom of this. Someone is going to pay," the Guard threatened, pointing the handle of his whip at Thomas and glaring around at them all. "Now, get back to work!"

They didn't wait to be asked twice but scuttled back to their duties.

Chapter 15

THE WASTELANDS

"Eew. What is that smell?" Freya wrinkled her nose in disgust.

Willow laughed. "That, my friend, is sulphur."

"It smells like …" Now, Freya wrinkled her brow, thinking.

"Rotten eggs. Yes, that's what sulphur smells like."

For the past five days, they'd been travelling the road towards Konia alongside the Helix River. Since leaving the outskirts of Beta, farmland and orchards had given way first to meadows of long grass with tiny white flowers, then bracken and brambles. But during the past day, they had been travelling through a more barren landscape: one of brown tussock, strewn with boulders on a carpet of reddish-brown dirt.

Now they had left the road and headed into the rolling hills. Standing atop a knoll, they surveyed the lay of the land. It spread out before them, the brown hills undulating on and on, as far as the eye could see. Here and there, wisps of steam drifted up from fissures in the ground. It was this steam that Freya could smell.

"Well, this is what we came here for. Let's do it," Freya said, marching towards the nearest tendril of steam. She knelt on the ground next to a patch of caked mud tinged with bright yellow crystals at the edge of the crevices where the steam drifted out. She dug out the tablet from her satchel, unwrapped it and held it carefully face-down over the steam. After a few moments, she pulled it back and inspected the face. Nothing.

"It didn't work," she said, disappointment in her voice.

Willow leant over her shoulder. "What's wrong?"

"I think it's not enough steam. Or maybe not enough sulphur in the steam," Freya said, standing up and eyeing the surrounding landscape. "Look, there's way more over there." She pointed off into the distance. "Let's go."

They headed towards a plume rising above a hill in the distance. The smell of sulphur grew stronger the closer they approached. They wove their way between the thigh-high tussocks. Initially, Freya had thought that the hostile environment would be devoid of life, but now she saw tiny brown lizards with a black stripe down their backs scuttling away at their approach. She jumped as a startled rabbit bolted from under her feet and darted off, zig-zagging between the grasses. And there! A mouse.

A screech sounded above her. She glanced up in time to see a hawk dive down and grab the mouse with its powerful talons. It flapped off, the tiny creature dangling from its claws.

Freya rubbed her sleeve across her brow. "It's hot out here."

"Sure is," replied Willow.

They trudged up another hill then stopped short, staring. Below them, a lake filled the basin formed by a ring of hills. Not a refreshing blue lake that beckoned one to jump in and swim. No, this lake was surrounded by oozing, bubbling grey mud. Great clouds of steam drifted from its surface. And it stank.

Freya pinched her nose. "Well, I think this should work," she said in a nasal voice.

Willow waved her hand under her nose, trying to make the smell go away. "I would say so. Be careful, Freya. It's steep here. Let's go that way." She pointed off to the right, where the hill sloped down to a small stream flowing out of the lake.

Freya nodded and threaded her way down, clutching at the rough grass to slow her descent. The acrid fumes stung her eyes and made them water. She blinked away her tears. With blurred vision, she stood on a rock. It turned under her foot, and before she knew it, she was sliding on her back down towards the mud.

Freya's scream was echoed by Willow. Freya flailed her arms wildly, trying to grab on to the tussocks. She pedalled her legs, but only succeeded in kicking gravel ahead of her. She slid feet-first into the steaming mud at the lake's edge and promptly came to a stop, the sticky mud up to her knees. "Help me!" she wailed.

Willow picked her way down as quickly as she could to where Freya lay. She skidded the last meter to land next to Freya's head. "Give me your hand," she urged. Bracing herself, she dragged Freya uphill, grunting with exertion.

Slowly, slowly, Freya came free of the mud.

"Are you alright?" Willow asked, anxiously.

Freya nodded. "Yeah. It was hot, but I don't think I'm burned." She stood shakily to her feet.

Suddenly, just metres away, a jet of steaming water spurted high into the air, spraying them with scalding drops. Freya got such a fright that she stepped backwards and sat down again with a thump. Clouds of steam billowed out and engulfed them.

"Quick, Freya! Your tablet," Willow wheezed, coughing and spluttering.

More by feel than sight, Freya grabbed her tablet, whipped

off the leather wrapping and held it out into the dense cloud. The geyser played for a few more minutes before dying away. As it did, the steam dissipated, and Freya could see her tablet once more. She pulled it back towards her and gazed at the surface. Sure enough, silvery writing had appeared. She read the words aloud:

> *Go up Helix River, to its source*
> *At the waterfall—a powerful force—*
> *Follow the sounds of birds up high*
> *Of honey bees buzzing as they fly*
>
> *When sunlight fades to shades of grey*
> *At dusk watch for nature's display*
> *From whence the cloud comes, will reveal*
> *The path which is elsewise concealed*

"By the Ancient," Willow breathed, "that's amazing! What number are you up to?"

"The previous verse ended at seventy," Freya obliged. "The next number we need is ninety-two." She counted the words in the new verses. "That's honey," she exclaimed. "And then the last number is ninety-nine." She counted on. "Sunlight," she announced. "Well, I already knew that words appear in sunlight. So, all we need to do is find the honey, and the tablet has told us where to find that."

"At the Helix waterfall," Willow mused. "It's been years since I've been there."

"You've been there? Do you remember there being lots of bees there?"

Willow thought for a moment. "No, can't say that I do. But

we should leave before that geyser decides to spray us again."

Freya nodded and looked at her tablet once more. The words were fading from its face. She wrapped it up and tucked it back into her satchel. Willow held out a hand. Freya took it and heaved herself upright. She brushed the dirt from the seat of her pants, adjusted the shield and tugged her tunic back into place. "Ready."

They walked back up the hill. At the top, they stopped and gazed about.

"Which way do we go? It all looks the same to me," Freya said in dismay.

Willow screwed up her eyes and studied the position of the sun. She turned her body so the sun was to her right, then pointed decisively in front of her. "That way. C'mon."

They set off, the red dirt crumbling underfoot as they passed. Every now and then Freya spotted a rabbit darting off or one of the tiny lizards sunning itself on a rock.

She heard a faint scraping sound and Willow stopped suddenly in her tracks in front of Freya, gesturing to Freya to stop moving. Willow was staring at the ground. "Shhh," she cautioned.

Freya peered carefully around Willow to see what had caused her alarm. There, slithering across their path was a big, fat, black snake. She froze, then took a cautious step backwards. Another step. Willow also slowly stepped backwards, never taking her eyes off the snake. Freya's heart hammered in her chest. She hoped the snake couldn't hear it. But the creature slithered off and disappeared under one of the tussocks. Freya let out the breath she'd been holding. "That was huge," she said.

Willow nodded. "I've never seen such a big one in my life! You okay?"

"Yeah. Just a little scared, I guess. Can we sit down for a bit, until I stop shaking?"

"Sure."

They sat down on a large smooth rock. Freya closed her eyes and spread her palms flat on the surface. Heat emanated from it, warming her. Gradually, her heart rate slowed and was no longer thumping in her ears. But what was that? Keeping her eyes shut, Freya listened intently. Yes, it was definitely something. A faint hum or vibration, at the very edge of her senses. One minute it was there, the next it was gone. The same sound she'd heard on her first morning in Tyrelia.

Freya's eyes popped open. "What is that?" she demanded.

"What?" Willow had shut her eyes too. She looked like she was nearly asleep.

"That noise. That humming, vibrating sound. Really faint."

Willow opened her eyes and glanced at Freya, frowning. "Oh yeah, that. I dunno."

"So, you can hear it then?"

"Yes, of course. But I don't know what it is. It's sort of always been there. Never really thought about it."

"Oh."

Willow stood up. "Come on, let's keep going. I'd rather not still be in the Wastelands by nightfall. Who knows what other creepy crawlies might find us?"

Freya shivered. It didn't bear thinking about. She hurried off after Willow.

Chapter 16

ARRESTED

A loud thumping on their door startled Thomas, Martha and Jack from their supper.

Thomas opened to the door to see four Guards with stern faces and long spears in their hands.

"You're required for questioning!" one commanded.

Martha shot an anxious glance at Jack, before they both stood up, their chairs scraping on the flagstone floor. Without talking, they followed Thomas out of the house. The Guards fell into formation, surrounding them.

They were marched to the Level One Office of the Master, within the entranceway under the Level One wall, where they had received their tokens and injections, the day they first entered the Golden City.

They were told to sit in the waiting room, then Thomas was taken separately into the small office. Two of the Guards stayed watching over Jack and Martha.

Jack heard sharp tones and muffled responses through the door, but he couldn't make out the words. What was Thomas telling them?

Could they deny all knowledge of Rube? Had anyone noticed them whispering to him? He thought they'd been discreet, but had they?

Now the voice sounded angry, and there was a banging noise, like a hand being thumped on the desk. Then it went very quiet. Jack strained his ears. He heard footsteps ringing out, then, *Smack! Smack!*

Next thing, the door swung open and a Guard came out supporting Thomas, who leaned heavily on him. One side of his face was bright red, and his left eye was starting to puff up.

Martha leapt to her feet. "Thomas!" she cried, reaching out to him.

The Guard nearby restrained her. "You're next," he said gruffly, and pushed her into the room. The door shut once more.

"Where are you taking him?" Jack demanded.

"Quiet!" the remaining Guard ordered.

Thomas moaned as he half stumbled and was half dragged out of the room.

Once again, Jack strained his ears to hear what was being said inside the interrogation room. A deep baritone rumble was followed by his mother's higher voice. "I don't know!" he clearly heard. She sounded agitated.

The door opened and his mother was led back out to sit next to Jack. It was his turn now.

With trepidation, he entered the room and the door was closed behind him.

"Stand there," the Guard instructed.

The same man who had given them their tokens the day they arrived was seated behind a desk. He glared at Jack with steely eyes.

"What do you know about that Transient?" he demanded.

Jack frowned. Then he remembered that the Guards referred to the Watchers as Transients. Even so, he resolved to tell them nothing. "I don't know anything about it, Sir," he responded respectfully. "As you know, I was busy fighting at the time. I only found out afterwards what had happened."

"Hmm." The man's eyes bored into Jack's, as if that would allow him to read Jack's mind. "Why did your father help him?"

"I dunno," Jack shrugged his shoulders and spread his hands out beside him. "Because he's a nice guy, I suppose?"

The man shook his head and an exasperated sound escaped his lips. "You are all most unhelpful. We are locking your father up for the time being. This might … ah … encourage you to remember some more details." The man continued to stare at Jack, gauging his reaction.

Jack clenched his jaw and stared back. "Thank you, Sir," he said.

"Dismissed," the man barked.

The Guard standing next to Jack gripped his arm above his elbow and marched him back out to the waiting room.

Martha leapt to her feet, relief sweeping across her features when she saw Jack was unharmed.

"Right, let's go," a Guard ordered, and they were escorted back to their house.

As they approached the front door, Jack saw their neighbour, Leena, peeking out from behind her curtain.

As soon as the Guards had left, she came hurrying over.

"What's happened?" she asked.

Martha wailed, "They've taken my Thomas!" She burst out crying.

Leena placed an arm around her friend's shoulders, drawing her into a hug. She patted her back. "Hush now, shhh, it'll be okay." She raised her eyebrows at Jack.

"I think I can tell you." Rube suddenly materialised, seated at their kitchen table.

"Rube!" they all exclaimed at once.

"Are you okay? How's your leg?" Jack asked.

Rube rubbed his hip. "I'm fine, thanks."

"What happened to your leg?" Leena demanded.

"Oh, a silly thing. I landed badly jumping off the cart I was hitching a ride on. It's not serious, but it was enough to prevent me being able to climb the tree."

Jack picked up the story. "Yes, so today when we got there, he was leaning against the trunk instead. So, Da and me were sort of trying to stop anyone from accidentally touching him, when this fella named Stefan started going on about how we always hog the best spot. He pushed Da, so I pushed him and next thing we were in a fight."

Leena's eyes were big. "Oh dear."

Martha spoke up. "I saw the fight start, but I didn't know what it was all about. Then the Guard went over to lash them with his whip. But Rube must've been standing in the way, and instead of the whip striking Jack and Stefan, it wrapped itself around Rube's arm. And then Rube became visible."

Leena gasped and clapped her hand to her mouth.

"I lost concentration," Rube apologised. "I immediately turned myself invisible again, but the darned thing was still wrapped around my arm."

"And of course," Martha explained, "it was still obvious where Rube was. So naturally, Thomas tried to unwrap it. I managed to distract the Guard by offering him a bun, which gave Thomas time to free Rube and for him to escape. But that's why the Guards came, and now they've locked Thomas up!"

Tears welled up in Martha's eyes once more, and she dabbed them with her hanky.

"No," Leena breathed. "Do you know for how long?"

Jack glanced at his mother. She was still wiping her eyes. "The Master's official is still suspicious that we know more than we told him—'cause of course, neither Ma nor I let on that we knew who Rube was." Jack inclined his head towards Rube. "We're pretty sure Da didn't say anything either, 'cause they beat him pretty bad. The official implied that they're going to keep him locked up until somebody 'remembers' something."

Leena thought a while, absorbing the information, then she looked at each of them in turn. "What are you going to do?"

Rube cleared his throat. "Well, it's no longer safe to meet me at the tree. Talking of which, I never got a chance to tell you the latest developments." He briefly touched Martha's arm. "My dear lady, I don't suppose I could bother you for a cup of tea while we talk?"

"Of course." Martha jumped at the suggestion to do something useful.

"I'll just go get Hank," Leena said. "He should be here for this. Won't be a minute."

By the time Martha had made the tea, Hank, Leena and young Sam were all crowded into her kitchen.

"We still haven't been able to contact Freya. But Thyst has discovered that she too, can see Tyrelia."

"By the Master! That's amazing," Leena exclaimed.

"How did she do it?" Jack demanded.

"We don't know," Rube sighed. "And Saff can still only see the Wall. There's still so much to figure out."

"And what are we going to do about my Thomas?" Martha asked.

Hank cleared his throat with a loud harrumph.

Everybody turned to look at him.

"There's something else you all need to know," he said, groping in his pocket. He pulled out a folded piece of paper. He opened it and spread it out on the table. They all crowded around. It was a poster of Rube. But this time there was a ten-thousand-unit reward attached.

Rube sat back in his seat. "This changes everything," he said, shaking his head. "It's becoming too risky for me to be in contact with you every day. I think it's best for everyone if I disappear for a bit."

"But how are we going to hear about whether Saff and Thyst find Freya?" Martha wailed.

"Well, by all accounts, there's not going to be much news. It's going to take Saff and Thyst five days or so to reach the Cave People. I suggest I come back here in a week's time."

Hank pursed his lips. "No, too dangerous to come here. I'm sure this house will be watched. How about you come to ours?" He glanced at Leena, who nodded in agreement.

"Yes, Rube. Much safer that way." She looked around the circle of faces.

"Where are you going to go?" Jack asked.

Rube shook his head slightly. "I think it's best for everyone if I don't tell you. That way, if the Guards decide to beat anyone again … well, you can't tell what you don't know, right?"

"Right," said Leena. "But tonight, you're staying at our place. And first, I'm going to cook you a proper dinner. You can go off and disappear tomorrow."

Rube leveraged himself upright, groaning as he did so. He rubbed his hip. "That, madam, sounds like an excellent idea," he said, smiling gratefully.

Chapter 17

RUBE'S DISCOVERY

As he had done several times already, Rube left the Golden City, trailing invisibly behind the Guards at the rear of the group of farmers, as they headed out into the fields at the third bell. But, once over the drawbridge, he peeled off to the left and skirted alongside the moat for fifteen minutes until he came to a small copse of trees. He crawled into the familiar hiding place and settled down to wait.

He puzzled over why it was that Freya and Thyst could no longer see the Wall. There must be a clue in the Prophecy. He ran through it in his mind:

That which was lost a millennium or more
Shall be found again by a Daughter of Yaw:
One who cannot see, yet is not blind —
If they seek, they shall find
The Path to set all mankind free
Straight through the heart of tyranny.
There is no need to see to believe;

There is more than one way the truth to perceive.

The key had to be in the last two lines. *There is no need to see to believe.* Well, that could refer to Freya being half blind. And she certainly had believed: not only in Tyrelia, but she'd also stubbornly believed in the Ancient, even though it was less than certain whether he was still alive or had ever existed.

But what about Thyst? She wasn't half blind. So maybe it was simply that she believed without seeing? But in that case, what did she believe that Saff didn't? Saff professed to believe in Tyrelia. So, what did that leave? Maybe it *was* the Ancient? Hmm, that was a possibility.

Then there was the very last line: *There is more than one way the truth to perceive.* What did that mean? Well, first, he supposed that one way of believing something to be true was actually seeing it. If you saw it, then it was real. Physical. You could touch it, feel it, smell it, taste it. But you could also believe something without seeing, feeling, smelling, tasting or hearing it. Without having proof. That was what people called 'faith'. So, what 'truth' had both Freya and Thyst come to believe in, without really having tangible proof? It *had* to be their belief that the Ancient was real.

Before he'd met Freya, when he'd lived in Yaw—what, was it only four weeks ago?—he'd been a librarian, working in the city archives. When Freya had first asked him about the Ancient, he'd had to confess that he had practically no knowledge. A thousand years ago, when the Master had raised the Wall in a single day and the Great Cleansing had begun, the Master's minions had relentlessly pursued the remaining Watchers in the Land. All but five Watchers had been destroyed. During that time of persecution, Watchers' houses had been torched and many documents lost. At one stage, he had discovered a dusty trunk in a forgotten corner of the Archives. Inside was a collection of very old parchments. Unfortunately, they were badly burnt, and he could not decipher much. But he did recall poring over them for weeks. One word-fragment he'd noticed immediately was 'yrelia', which he was now certain referred to *Tyrelia*. But in the end, it was just a word here and a word there, and not much meaning was to be obtained.

It occurred to him that there was possibly only one place in the whole of Medar where he might find reference to the Ancient. But it would be risky. Oh, so risky! His heart started thumping in his chest at the thought of it. But the more he thought about it, the more certain he became that it was his only option. He would discuss it with Saff and Thyst at sunset tonight.

~

Concealed within the cluster of bushes just before sunset, Rube gazed into the swirling shades of red emanating from the stone on the flat of his palm. The various tones formed themselves into Saff's face.

"Saff," he said urgently. "There's been a change of plan."

"What's happened?"

"Well, it's a bit of a long story, but I injured my leg, and I couldn't climb the tree. A Guard lashed out his whip to break up a fight between Jack and some other fellow—I can't remember his name—but instead the whip wrapped around my arm, and in my surprise, I let my invisibility slip. They saw me, Saff."

"By the Land! But you escaped?"

"Yes. Luckily, Thomas managed to free me from the wretched thing, and I ran away. But as a result, the Guards have locked Thomas up, and there's a bounty poster out. There's a ten-thousand-unit reward on me too, now."

Saff chuckled. "Between us, we're quite valuable."

"This is no time for jests," Rube reprimanded. "I can no longer risk my daily rendezvous with Freya's family. I need to make myself scarce for a while. Saff, do you believe in the Ancient?"

Saff's mouth gaped open. This sudden change of tack left him confused. "Huh? Why do you ask?"

"Well, do you?" Rube asked impatiently.

"I … uh … I don't know," Saff finally responded.

"Just as I thought," Rube said, frowning.

"What's this about?" Saff demanded.

"I have a theory," Rube replied, "about why both Freya and Thyst can no longer see the Wall. I think it's because they believe without seeing."

"What?"

"You know. The Prophecy. *There is no need to see to believe; There is more than one way the truth to perceive.*"

"Aah … and?"

Rube took a deep breath. "I think the reason that both Freya and Thyst can see Tyrelia is because they believe in the Ancient. Even though they have no physical evidence that he exists."

"Oh."

"But I want to test my theory. I think I need to search for some records about the Ancient."

"I thought you'd done that and concluded that no such records exist?"

"That's right. No records in any libraries that I've had access to."

"So … what are you thinking?"

"I'm going to try to find the Master's library. In the Golden

City."

"You're WHAT?" This from both Saff and Thyst.

Rube nodded. "I've got to try. And who knows. Going higher into the Golden City might be the safest place for me right now."

Saff shook his head. "I don't know. Maybe. But … what if you can't pass through the Level Two gate? Or Level Three … ?" Saff's voice trailed off.

"There's only one way to find out." Rube said with determination. "I'm going to give myself a week. Then, if I'm able, I'll come outside the city and try and contact you again at sunset on the seventh day. I have to try."

"Okay, Rube. We'll talk to you in a week then. Good luck, my friend."

Chapter 18

VIBRATIONS

Freya and Willow had spent the night on the side of the road in a small copse of trees. Now they continued on the road towards Konia, the Helix River on their left and the Wastelands to their right.

"So, how long do you reckon it'll take us to travel to Konia?" Freya asked.

Willow wrinkled her brow. "Usually it takes about two weeks from Konia to Beta with the sheep. It would be a lot quicker without them. We've been travelling for six days already. But, of course, we made a bit of a detour into the Wastelands. So, I'm guessing another six days. I'll have a better idea when we arrive at the Law Pillar."

"Law Pillar? What's that?"

Willow turned to Freya and gestured above her head. "You know, a tall thing, round. Made of stone."

Freya nodded enthusiastically. "Yes, I saw one when I first entered Tyrelia. It had the *Laws of Tyrelia* on it."

"Mmm, that's right. So, there's pillars like that everywhere. I guess the Ancient wants to make sure that we remember the

Laws." Willow pulled a face.

"Why are you grimacing? The Laws seem all right to me."

"*Follow the Rules*," Willow chanted. "It's so … authoritarian." She cut her eyes at Freya. "Don't you have Laws in Medar?"

Freya pursed her lips. "Well, not on pillars like here. But everyone knows that you'd better do what the Master and his Guards want, or else."

"Or else what?"

Freya shivered. "Or you get taken away and never seen again. Probably killed. Like my birth mother."

Willow stopped in her tracks. "What?" She stared at Freya, stunned.

Freya shrugged. "I never knew this until a month ago, when I found out I was adopted. Apparently, right after I was born, a Guard came bursting into our house, grabbed her and threw her in the Chasm."

Willow looked aghast. "Who would do such a thing?" she demanded.

"The Master," Freya muttered. "I suppose that's what happens when you don't have Laws like *Put others first* and *Use your gifts for good*."

"Talking of which," Willow pointed. "Look! There it is."

Freya gazed ahead. It stood off to their left. From this distance, the structure looked smooth and unmarked. But as they drew closer, Freya saw strange shadows on its surface, which, as they neared, refined into words carved deeply into the stone surface.

Freya shivered, rubbing her ear. "That humming is really strong here."

Willow looked at her quizzically. "No more than usual."

Freya shook her head. "No, it's like the air is pulsing. Can't you feel it?" Freya walked towards the pillar, her arms outstretched in front of her, as if she were sleep walking.

"Freya!" Willow called. Her voice was muffled. "What are you doing?"

The air around Freya hummed and throbbed. It filled her senses, soothing her, caressing her. Freya smiled.

Then everything happened at once.

Willow grabbed Freya's arm, pulling her backwards. Then they were both falling. The throbbing hum engulfed them. They landed in a heap. The humming stopped abruptly.

Freya looked around her, dazed. "Where are we?"

Willow lay on the ground beside her, her eyes shut. She moaned. Her eyes fluttered open. "What *was* that?" she groaned. She pushed herself to a sitting position and looked around her. "Oh!" she exclaimed. "We're in Konia."

They were in a cobbled plaza, next to a pillar. A Law Pillar. Several people stood nearby, clutching at each other, shocked looks on their faces. "By the Ancient," one muttered.

Willow stood up and brushed herself down. "No," she replied cheerily, "it's just me. Willow." She proffered her hand to Freya and pulled her up. "And my friend Freya."

They both turned to stare at the pillar. "I think," Willow said slowly, "that we just travelled two hundred rata." She turned to Freya, grinning. "Just like that." She clicked her fingers. "That was *cool!* How did you do it?"

Freya shook her head. "I don't know, Willow. Another mystery. One more thing to ask the Ancient when we find him."

"Well, in the meantime, let's go home. I feel a nice bath and decent meal are in order."

Chapter 19

JACK'S BET

At last Saturday arrived. Despite his father being locked up, Jack could barely contain his excitement. He wasn't sure if he was more excited about his fight or about placing a bet. Maybe, just maybe, he'd be able to bribe the Guards with his winnings to let his da go?

He'd gone ahead of his ma and the others, making the excuse that Orn had asked him to be there early. He pressed through the crowds and once through the gate looked around eagerly.

"Hey, Jack!" Straw hailed him.

"Straw! Hay! Good to see you." Jack strode over and high-fived them.

They headed off to the opposite end of the arena from where the wrestling ring was, towards a large tent. Several people and Guards were already streaming towards it and the ale tent next door.

Straw opened the flap of the tent and stepped inside. Jack followed him in, then stopped short, staring around. A counter ran along the length of the back of the tent. It had partitions every metre or so, forming booths. Behind each booth stood a bookie. Queues were starting to form in front of each booth. Some people pushed past Jack and Straw.

"Out of the doorway," a man growled as he passed.

Jack took a few steps forward then stopped to inspect the boards along one wall. More boards ran the length of the other two walls. Draws for all the competitions were pinned on the boards. Signs hanging above the boards proclaimed which competition was displayed below it. He gazed around at the signs and spotted the one for 'Wrestling' at the opposite end of the tent. He strode over, Straw and Hay in his wake. They all studied the draws.

"Hey, Jack. Check out the odds against you winning your matches," Straw exclaimed.

"Yeah, well, it's because I've moved up to the next round," Jack responded defensively.

The book makers had indeed rated Jack very unlikely to win. On the other hand, there was a tidy sum to be made should he win.

"What are you going to do?" Hay asked. "You'd be a fool to bet on yourself."

Jack sighed. "Yeah, I know." He studied the odds. "Looks like that chap called Simon is the favourite. I suppose it would be safest to bet on him."

Straw clapped Jack on the back. "I've decided on my bet. You ready to place yours?"

Jack nodded. He followed Straw to the nearest empty booth. Straw placed his bet then stepped aside. Now it was Jack's turn. He stepped up to the table.

"What'll it be?" the bookie asked pleasantly.

Jack didn't know what came over him. His heart thumped in his ears and tiny droplets of sweat broke out on his brow. "I'd like to bet the lot on Jack from Nob in the Wrestling lightweight division two match," he heard himself say.

The bookie swept Jack's hard-earned money towards himself before making some notes in his book. He counted out the money and carefully entered the amount next to his other entries. "You'll make a pretty packet if that Jack wins," he commented as he handed Jack a slip of paper with his betting number on it.

"Thanks," Jack mumbled as he took it and turned away.

"What happened?" Straw elbowed him in the side. "I thought you were going to bet on that Simon guy?"

Jack shrugged. "Dunno. Changed my mind, I guess. C'mon, let's go. I've got some winning to do."

They hurried out of the tent and across the arena to the wrestling ring. Good, his mother wasn't there yet. Orn was though.

"Where 'ave you been? Hurry and warm up," he growled.

Jack obliged, but he couldn't concentrate and kept on thinking about his bet. What if he did win? He'd probably make enough money to bribe the Guards *and* buy his way up to Level Two tomorrow!

Shortly, his ma, Hank, Leena and Sam turned up. Martha marched straight towards Jack. His hand went guiltily to his pocket where his betting slip was tucked away. Had she guessed?

"Jack, I'm so sorry, love, I've got to go serve ale. We might hear something more about Rube … or your da. Sorry I'm going to miss your fight again." She gave him a big hug.

Jack breathed a sigh of relief. "It's okay, Ma, I understand."

She pecked him on the cheek and hurried off with Leena.

Before long a bell sounded, and the opening announcement

rang throughout the arena. Jack tried to focus on the division two matches, but his thoughts kept on drifting to the betting tent and a stab of excitement shot through him.

"Jack!" Orn shouted again.

Hank stood in front of him, waving a hand in front of Jack's eyes. "Are you all right?" he asked.

Jack shook his head slightly, to clear it. "Sorry, yeah. Just nerves," he lied. He'd been lost in his dreams.

Orn thumped him on the back. "Nerves are good. Keep you sharp. Right, you're up. Off you go." He pushed Jack into the ring.

Jack stood facing his opponent in the neutral position. He stared at the dark-haired man. Was he Simon? He didn't know. He should've studied all his opponents prior to the match. *Focus, Jack,* he told himself.

Next thing, he was flat on his back, so winded that he couldn't move.

"One, two, three!" The referee counted off the seconds. Jack had lost.

He tried to push himself up, but a stab of pain shot through his back. He moaned.

Orn and Hank rushed over. "Easy, easy," Orn soothed.

A medic arrived and pushed the men aside. He felt Jack's neck, got him to raise his arms and legs, and wiggle his fingers. After a few anxious minutes, Jack rolled on to his side and stood up.

Supported by the medic, he slowly walked over to where Orn was waiting.

"He's strained his back, pinched a nerve. He'll be all right but needs to rest it now. Under no circumstances can he fight any more today," the medic advised Orn.

"Oh, too bad," Orn exclaimed. He slipped his arm under Jack's and helped him over to the bleachers. "Looks like your nerves got to you, Jack," he chided. "Never mind though, it could've been a lot worse."

Jack disagreed. He'd just bet all his money that he'd win. But now he'd not only lost the match, he'd lost all his money. How was he going to get his da back now?

Chapter 20

SUPERBIA

Rube stood invisibly in front of the gate to Level Two. This was it. This would be the test of whether his Tyrelian blood would withstand the forces of this gate. Presumably, if he couldn't pass, then he'd die and become visible again. What a commotion that would cause.

He stood there for ten full minutes, staring at the gate. There was writing along the top of the archway, engraved into the stone blocks: S U P E R B I A. Huh, what did that mean? He'd have to look it up … if he ever survived this ordeal. He took a deep breath. He couldn't delay any longer. He stepped forward.

"Hey, you!" A Guard marching back and forth behind the parapet above the gate called out, staring straight at him.

Rube froze and glanced down at himself. No, he was still invisible.

"What're you doing?"

A voice directly behind him squeaked, "Who, me?"

Rube nearly jumped out of his skin, so close was the man. In his concentration, he hadn't even noticed him.

"N … nothing," the man stammered. "Just resting in the

shade."

"Well, go rest somewhere else," the Guard commanded.

"Yessir." The man scurried off.

Phew, that was close.

And now was as good a time as any. Whilst the Guard was still somewhat distracted by the other man, Rube quickly but quietly walked up to the gate … under the gate … so far so good … and out the other side. He stopped and patted himself. He couldn't help it. Yes, he was still in one piece. He started walking again, his heart hammering in his chest. Nothing had happened. He was through.

He walked quickly over to a wall and slumped against it, breathing deeply. He hadn't realised he was so nervous. A bead of sweat trickled down his brow. He wiped it off. He pushed himself away from the wall and set off once more.

He looked around with interest. Was this Level different to Level One? Was it really worth paying all that gold to buy your way up? From what he could see, the buildings looked pretty similar. The streets were quiet for, of course, the inhabitants were at work or school. Up ahead he heard voices. He quickened his pace. As he rounded a corner, he discovered the source of the voices: a group of mothers with their babies in a small grassy area, under some trees.

"Well, of course, my wee George is only a week old, but I swear he smiled at me this morning. He's so advanced," one crooned.

Another rolled her eyes. "Next you'll be claiming that he'll be rolling at two months old. Now, my Netta is only four months old, and she did her first roll yesterday. *That's* advanced."

A third one snorted. "That's nothing. My fella, Bertie, here, he's *sitting by himself* at four months old. You're such a smart boy," she crooned at the infant sleeping in his pram.

Rube shook his head as he moved on. What was it, some sort of baby competition? Really.

The main road wound its way gradually higher, round and round the conical city. After an hour, he came across several young men loitering outside a building chewing tobacco. It must be time for the morning tea break.

"Did you see my match at the Games yesterday?" one asked.

The other two shook their heads. "How did you do?"

"I won," the first announced smugly. "Of course."

"Oh, well the reason I missed it was because I was too busy winning my own match. And wrestling is *so* much more difficult than boxing. More refined. Therefore, my win is better than yours," the second man retorted.

The third young man spat a big gob of tobacco on the ground. "Winning a wrestling or boxing match is easy," he drawled. "Now, doing what I did, that's better still."

"Oh, do enlighten us, Baz."

Baz stuck his nose in the air. "I used my intellect to study the odds ... and I bet on your matches." He grinned. "That's right, lads. I won gold yesterday. More gold than either of you. So, I win. I'm better than you both."

Rube left them to it. Everyone seemed intent on proving that they were better than everyone else. What a waste of time.

Another hour later he reached the Level Three gateway. He stopped to study it. Sure enough, this one also had a word engraved above it: A V A R I T I A. He didn't know what that meant either. He tucked the sword away. Right, now for the gate. More confident this time, he walked towards it ... into its shadow ... and passed through without incident. He sagged with relief.

Then he straightened his back and looked around. Directly opposite the gateway was a row of houses. In front of them, the road stretched to his left and to his right, both heading slightly uphill. Which way should he go? Off to his right, he heard faint cheering and clapping. That sounded interesting. He headed towards it.

Before long, the road opened into a small plaza. A well stood in the centre of the space, but all the activity was focused around the edges: restaurants and bars occupied every side of the square. Brightly coloured awnings shaded tables and chairs, and music drifted from various establishments. It was after the tenth bell, and the inhabitants were gathering to have a drink after a hard day's work.

A large crowd was gathered at one particular bar. This was the source of cheering and clapping Rube had heard. He drifted towards it, careful not to touch anyone.

He skirted around the edge of the crowd, trying to see what was happening. He heard a rattling sound, followed by a thump. "Two sixes!" someone shouted triumphantly. Half of the crowd cheered, whilst others hissed. Rube managed to catch a glimpse of two men seated at a table. They were playing dice. One man had rather a lot of coins on his side of the table, whilst the other had only one.

The one with a single coin rubbed his hand sharply through his thinning black hair. "I'm done," he said, pushing his chair back.

"No," the other said. "You can win it back. One more try, Manny. Come on, it's a bit of fun."

"For you maybe," Manny shot back. "You've fleeced me, Pablo. Now let's call it quits."

Pablo's eyes glittered. "Oho, Manny's yellow. Does Francesca know you're yellow inside?" he taunted.

Manny pulled his chair back in to the table. "I'm not yellow," he said defiantly.

"Well, prove it then," Pablo shot back.

Manny grabbed the dice and shoved them back into the cup. He shook it furiously then tipped the dice onto the table. They spilled out. A one and a three. Manny sucked his breath in.

Pablo smiled. "My turn." He rolled the dice. A two and a four. "Looks like it's just my lucky day," he announced cheerfully, scraping Manny's last coin towards him. "Say, I don't suppose you want to try and win it back … you could bet that nice jacket you're wearing."

Manny just stared at Pablo. "Now you're getting greedy. I'm done." He shoved his chair backwards and shouldered his way through the crowd out of the square. He brushed past Rube but didn't notice that he'd touched someone invisible.

Rube hurried away before someone else touched him.

He wound his way up the level until he found himself outside the Level Four gate. He stopped and studied it. This one bore the inscription I R A. Interesting. So that was *SUPERBIA, AVARITIA* and *IRA*. He wondered what they all meant. He hardly hesitated before walking through the gateway. As before, nothing happened. Good.

By now it was dusk. Rube found a narrow alley that was completely in shadow in the middle section. He slumped down against it, rubbing his hip as he did so. After having a bite to eat and some gulps of water, he leaned his head back against the wall. Before long, he drifted off to sleep.

Chapter 21

A RULE

They had only stayed one night with Willow's parents. It had not gone well.

After landing unexpectedly in Konia, Freya had followed Willow to her parents' home. She was still in a daze from travelling between the Law Pillars. Her hair was matted from sleeping on the side of the road and her trousers were caked in dried, smelly mud.

Willow knocked on her parents' door. "Hello?" she hollered.

A tall woman with blonde hair opened the door. Her eyes widened in delight, then she gathered Willow into a hug. "Willow! What a surprise. We weren't expecting you for a few more days yet," she exclaimed.

"I know, Mother, but here I am. Oh, and this is my friend, Freya." She gestured to Freya, who was hanging back behind her.

Willow's mother's smile faded as her eyes settled on Freya. Frowning, she spoke to Willow in hushed tones, but Freya heard her clearly. "Willow, honey, you can't keep befriending strangers," she admonished. "What if she's dangerous?"

Willow guffawed. "Don't be silly. Freya's really nice. And besides, she's special. She's from the Hole and she's got a magic shield."

This information apparently did not impress Willow's mother as, shooting another look at Freya, she grabbed her daughter's arm and pulled her inside, closing the door behind them.

Freya stared at the closed door. The voices were muffled now, and she could only make out a word here and there: 'Hole', 'dark' and 'untrustworthy'. Freya turned and sat down on the step. Then Willow's voice, shrill with anger. Next, a male voice joined the conversation.

Suddenly, the door was locked.

Freya jerked her head up. Huh? She half turned towards the door. She heard thumping sounds and raised voices. Willow's voice. Receding into the house. Then a door slammed somewhere inside. Silence.

Slowly, Freya stood up, her shoulders slumped. She was tired, so tired. She looked left and right, before stumbling around the side of the house and collapsing between a bush and a lean-to containing a stack of firewood. Sobbing, she rocked herself to sleep.

Sometime in the black of night, she awoke to an insistent whispering, "Freya! Freya!" It was Willow.

Freya bolted upright, stiff and sore from having fallen asleep slouched against the woodshed. "I'm here," she called cautiously.

"Oh, Freya, I thought you'd gone." Willow's voice was urgent. "But I'm glad you're still here. I'm so sorry about my parents. They don't understand." She shook her head. "They think that their friends are going to disown them if they find out that they've associated with someone from the Hole. Stupid." She hissed indignantly.

"Oh." Freya didn't know what else to say.

"C'mon," Willow urged. "Come inside and let's get you cleaned up."

"Are you sure?" Freya ventured. "Your parents …"

"They're asleep," Willow assured her. "Come on. We'll sneak out first thing, before they wake up. They'll never know."

~

Now, three days later, Freya and Willow worked their way upstream along the Helix River towards the Majestic Mountains. The ground rose steadily underfoot as they climbed higher and higher. After days of walking amongst rolling foothills, the way ahead was now blocked by a sheer cliff, as the Helix tumbled through a gorge in the valley below. Their route took them along an exposed path around the bluff.

"Hey, Freya, come and check out this view," Willow called, as they emerged from the shrubbery. She shaded her eyes against the glare as she gazed about her.

Freya came to stand beside her. "Wow," she said, sucking in her breath.

Tyrelia lay spread before them like a giant painting.

"Look," Willow pointed far below them. "There's Konia. And see that reddish-brown area? That's the Wastelands."

Freya squinted. "Oh yes, I think I can see that geyser." Her eyes were drawn to an enormous grey, murky area beyond the Wastelands. It seemed to stretch along the entire horizon. Involuntarily, she shivered. "Is that … ?" Her voice trailed off.

Beside her Willow nodded. "Yes. The Hole."

"Medar." Freya hugged herself, as if for comfort. "I had no idea … it's completely covered in cloud. No wonder I thought it was so bright here."

"Doesn't really look very appealing, does it?"

Freya shook her head slowly. "No, not at all."

With a shiver, she tore her gaze away. "Can we go now, please?"

~

"How far to the waterfall, Willow?" Freya asked between bites of a delicious apple.

Willow tossed her core off into the bushes that lined the path. "Another two days. First, we need to cross the river. We should reach my brother Alex tomorrow. Then I think it's another day from there, depending on how long it takes us to find Alex."

Freya stopped in her tracks. "Shouldn't we have crossed the river way back when the banks were lower?"

The path had climbed steadily since leaving Konia and the Helix River had dropped away farther and farther below them on their left into a deep ravine. They could clearly hear it chattering and splashing over rocks and boulders a hundred metres below them.

Willow grinned, showing a flash of white teeth. "No, silly. There's a bridge. Come on. It can't be far now."

They set off once more. The gravel path was smooth and wide, but not busy. They had seen only a few people in their three days of travel so far. It was another fine day and, although the sun was hot overhead, Freya had borrowed one of Willow's old caps which shaded her face and reduced the glare.

To their right, a steep bank covered in trees and grasses towered above their heads. To their left stretched a wide verge with stones, dusty grasses and some sort of weed that grew up to Freya's thighs, covered in tiny yellow flowers. Beyond that, the cliff dropped away. They couldn't see the river from the path unless they stepped closer to the edge and craned their necks to look down.

The opposite bank of the river was a sheer cliff. It reminded Freya of looking across the Chasm and seeing the Wall.

But all thoughts of the Chasm and the Wall were driven from her mind the moment they rounded a bend in the path: the ravine opened out to a wide valley with green pasturelands up on a plateau on the opposite bank. A slender suspension bridge spanned the ravine.

"There you go," Willow announced, bowing dramatically to Freya.

"You're amazing, Willow. I wish you were my guide. Oh, hang on a minute, you *are* my guide!"

They both laughed as they walked up to the bridge. There was a sign hanging above the entrance. It read:

ONE PERSON AT A TIME

"You first, Freya," Willow said graciously. "After all, *Others first*—that's the Law."

Freya stepped up to the beginning of the bridge and stood looking down the length of it. She grabbed the rope handrails and shook them. They felt strong and sturdy. A slight tremor rippled the length of the bridge. She poked the timber planks with her foot. They creaked slightly, but apart from that there was hardly any movement.

"Well, off you go," Willow said.

The last bridge she'd crossed had been across the Chasm. That one hadn't even had handrails. But then again, it hadn't moved and swayed. Not wanting Willow to think she was a scaredy-cat, Freya took a deep breath and, gripping the ropes tightly in each hand, she stepped onto the bridge. That was all right. She took a few more steps. The bridge swayed. She focused on the far end of the bridge and, walking slowly and deliberately, before she knew it she was well out into the ravine.

"This isn't so bad," she shouted over her shoulder.

Suddenly, the bridge jolted.

"Help!" Freya screamed, holding on even tighter to the ropes and squatting down on the bridge.

The whole structure started swaying wildly. Freya looked under her arm to see what had caused the tumult and saw Willow stomping towards her with a big grin on her face.

"Stop it!" Freya called out to her.

Something very strange was happening to the bridge. Even though it was only Willow stomping along the bridge, the ripples seemed to be strengthening.

Freya looked ahead of her once more. The bridge was alive, with ripples surging along its length to the other end like a giant serpent. Suddenly, she felt very ill. She lost her grip and fell against the latticework of ropes between the handrails and the planks. She rolled to one side and her arm flopped through between the ropes. Her weight was causing the gaps between the ropes to widen. The knots weren't very tight. She was slipping …

"Freya, I've got you!" Willow yelled, heaving Freya by her belt on to the deck of the bridge.

Freya lay on her back with her eyes squeezed shut. The bridge was still swaying side to side. After a few minutes, she opened her eye.

Willow was kneeling beside her, looking concerned. "Are you okay? I'm so sorry."

"What were you thinking?" Freya reprimanded her. "The

sign said *One Person at a Time.*"

"I know," Willow said in a small voice, "but I didn't think *that* would happen. I was just having a bit of fun."

The swaying came to a stop, and Freya slowly sat up. She looked Willow in the eye. "Yes, well, maybe now you realise that there's a reason for Rules."

"You're right, Freya. I'm sorry. Will you forgive me?"

Freya sighed. "Of course. Can we get off this bridge now, please?"

"Sure, you go first."

Freya shook her head. "Umm, no thanks. I think I'll wait here until you're off."

"Fair enough." Willow carefully stood up and, trying to make the bridge move as little as possible, made her way to the other end.

Only after Willow was completely off the bridge did Freya stand up and follow her. When she got to the other end, she stepped gratefully onto the grass and stared around. It was as though a whole section of the cliff had slipped half-way down to form a flat, grassy shelf this side of the river. About fifty metres away, the cliff continued to tower above them, creating a sheltered, peaceful space. The air was very still. Small insects buzzed and butterflies fluttered from flower to flower.

"Phew, it's hot," Freya commented, running her finger along the neckline of her tunic to pull the clinging fabric off her skin. She tipped her drinking skin to her lips and took a big swig of water, then rolled up her sleeves. "Oh," she exclaimed.

"What's wrong?" Willow asked, alarmed.

"Look." Freya held out her arm to Willow, palm up.

"By the Ancient! That's amazing." Willow stretched out her hand and traced the vein running up Freya's forearm with her finger. There was an unmistakeable glow about Freya's skin. It wasn't as radiant as Willow's, but it was more than it had been.

"How do you think it's happened?"

"I don't know. Maybe it's just being in Tyrelia."

"I wish there was someone we could ask. I'm sure the Ancient would know."

Willow laughed.

"What?" Freya demanded. "Why is that funny?"

"Oh, I'm sorry, Freya. But how would we ask the Ancient?"

"I don't know. But the clues in the tablet are leading us somewhere. I'm sure part of that will give us some answers. I don't know how, but I trust the tablet. After all, it led me safely out of Medar. Maybe it will lead me to the Ancient."

"Maybe," Willow agreed.

They set off once more.

Chapter 22

JACK'S DILEMMA

Jack paced back and forth in their kitchen, thinking. Martha had slipped into depression once more. It was worse than when they'd first moved to the Golden City and had thought Freya was dead. At least back then Thomas had been there to support and comfort Jack's mother. But Thomas was locked up somewhere. It was only him and his ma now. It was up to him to do something.

After work, they'd tried to find out where Thomas was being kept, but the Guards were most unhelpful. It would be very handy having the gift of invisibility, right now. Actually, thinking about it, Rube really should have stuck around. Scouted out where Thomas was. Helped them to free him. It wasn't right that he just disappeared and left them to it. How dare he, really.

It was all very well for *him*. He could up and leave the Golden City any time he wanted! But Thomas? No, not only could they not go further than five kilometres beyond the city wall at the best of times, but now he was locked away—somewhere horrible, no doubt.

The more he thought about it, the angrier he got. He clenched his fists and kicked the table leg.

His poor ma. She was heartbroken. He didn't know how much longer she would hold it all together. She'd stopped eating and had dark circles under her eyes. He had to get his da back, and soon.

But how? There was only one way that he could think of. It would mean betraying Rube. But if that's what he had to do to reunite his parents … then did he really have a choice? And the reward … well, that would be a bonus. No! He pushed the thought away. He wouldn't be doing it for the money, he would be doing it for his parents. Sometimes, the means justified the end. If he had to sacrifice Rube to free his father, then so be it.

Only problem was, he didn't know where Rube was. A smile crept across his face. But he *would* know where he'd be in a week's time.

Jack stopped pacing and rested his hands on the back of a chair. He nodded to himself. He had no choice. It was his only option.

Chapter 23

HIGHER AND HIGHER

Rube woke early the next morning, stiff and sore. He'd slid down the wall during the night and had ended up in an awkward position. He groaned as he stood up and massaged his hip. He'd thought it before, but he really was too old for this. After a bite to eat, he set off once more.

He had not gone far when he heard raised voices. They were coming from up ahead. Even though he was invisible, he poked his head cautiously around the corner.

A woman and a man stood inches from each other outside the open door of a house. Their faces were red and scrunched up, their noses practically touching. Their eyes bulged and their fists were clenched as they spat insults at each other.

"You're useless," the woman screamed. "We're supposed to be saving money to buy up to Level Five, and you've gone and blown it all on new shoes. Shoes!"

"I work hard," the man responded. "I deserve to spend money on myself sometimes. And what about you? You're forever spending money on so-called beauty treatments. I don't know why you bother, they don't seem to work very well."

The woman narrowed her eyes, pressed her lips together and took a step back. She raised her hand and swiped a stinging slap across the man's face. "How dare you!" She spun away and ran back into the house, slamming the door behind her.

The man's eyes watered as he stumbled backwards from the blow, clutching at his cheek. He stared at the closed door for a few seconds, before turning on his heel and striding off down the street.

Rube trailed behind the man at a distance. It seemed as good a route as any. Before long, the smell of freshly baked bread assailed his nostrils. Mmm. The man ahead of him stopped and lifted his head, sniffing. He abruptly crossed the road and entered the bakery shop. The smell drew Rube like a magnet and, without thinking, he too crossed the street. He peered through the window. It was only a small shop. A sour-looking fellow stood behind a counter on whose surface were arrayed plates of scones, muffins and pastries. A shelf behind him displayed row upon row of loaves of bread: round ones, long ones, white ones, brown ones. Some with sesame seeds, some with poppy seeds. Rube's mouth watered.

Five customers were inside. Maybe he could sneak inside while one of them was coming out? He sidled up to the doorway. Someone was coming out now. A woman. The door swung outwards and the woman stepped out. She had a big basket on her arm. Rube stepped quickly backwards to avoid being struck in the stomach by it. By the time he'd recovered, the door had closed. Bother.

It was a full two minutes before the next person came out. Rube braced himself. Suddenly, he heard raised voices.

"But I wanted that cream bun," a woman said.

"Too bad. I was here first," a man snapped.

"What happened to gallantry?"

"Ha! Good luck finding any of that in Level Four." The door swung open and a man stormed out, clutching a cream bun in his hand.

Rube seized his chance and tried to slip inside before the door closed. The shop was dim, and Rube didn't see the woman until it was too late. *Smack!* He banged straight into her. The impact sent him tumbling backwards. He fell heavily onto the pavement. He sat there, winded.

The woman squeaked and dropped her basket, spilling bread buns of various shapes and colours onto the floor. One rolled out of the door as it closed ... and promptly vanished into thin air.

"What a stupid thing to do, dropping all your buns."

"It wasn't my fault. The door closed on me or something. Give me some fresh ones," the woman demanded.

"No way. You dropped them. You want some more, you pay for them."

"No!" The woman turned to another customer in the shop. "You saw. It wasn't my fault. Tell him."

"I dunno," a woman's voice mumbled. "I didn't see anything. Just you dropping the basket."

"How dare you take his side. You're so weak, Hilda. Just like your eyesight. You're all useless!" The door banged open and the woman stormed out.

Rube had regained his breath. He slowly got to his feet and stood staring at the woman's retreating back. Why was everyone so angry here? Shaking his head, he set off once more, taking a big bite out of the fresh bun as he went.

The streets climbed steadily higher at the same gradient as the previous levels. After about an hour, he arrived at the Level Five gateway. He peered at the letters: L U X U R I A. Hmm.

He glanced briefly around him before hurrying unnoticed through the gate. Once through, he stopped and looked around. There was something different about this Level. What was it? He sniffed. Perhaps it was that faint scent of musk? Out of the corner of his eye, he saw something fluttering. He turned his head. Red gauze curtains floated on the breeze out of a nearby doorway. A deep baritone voice rumbled, followed by the tinkle of female laughter.

Rube started towards the fluttering curtains, but then noticed another open door further down, also with curtains fluttering. How strange. Curious now, he picked up his pace. As he approached the second doorway, he heard faint music coming from somewhere up ahead.

He rounded the corner and just stopped himself from bumping into a man who was leaning up against the wall. Rube held his breath and stepped quietly across the road.

"Are you there, lover boy?" A woman's sultry voice issued from the opening.

The man immediately straightened up, smiling. He cleared his throat and tugged at his collar. "Sure am, sweet thing." He stepped towards the doorway.

A bare arm snaked out, beckoning. The nails were painted bright red, and gold bracelets jangled softly. Rube stared at it, transfixed.

The hand grabbed the man's collar and pulled him inside. "C'mon, you. Are you ready for a good time?"

Rube hurried away. By the Master, it was only just after the third bell! Did these Level Five inhabitants not have any work to do?

Rube walked on and on. Every now and then, he noticed the same musky fragrance, or saw the same red curtains in certain houses. It was strange that he hadn't seen this on any other levels. Just this one. Like it was specific to this Level. Rube stopped in his tracks. Could it be? Did each Level have its own … emotion? Mood? He recalled how on Level Four everyone had seemed so angry. And here it seemed to all be about lust. Maybe that's what the words meant over each archway? What was this one again? *LUXURIA*. Maybe that was another word for *lust*. And maybe *IRA* meant *anger*. Of course! Another word for anger was *ire*. Perhaps the Level Three word *AVARITIA* had something to do with gambling, and the Level Two word, *SUPERBIA*, with boasting?

With renewed purpose, he wound his way up the city, towards the next gate. Finally, after another hour, he was there. Panting slightly from exertion, he leaned his hand against the wall as he mopped his brow with the other. He studied the Level Six Gate: *G U L A*. Raising his eyebrows, he quietly walked through the gate. Time to find out what *GULA* meant.

The minute he passed through the gate, the most delicious smell assailed his nostrils. Roast meat. Herbs and spices. Tangy fruits. His stomach rumbled loudly. Rube pressed his hand to it and glanced around anxiously. Thankfully nobody was near enough to have heard it. By now it was past midday and, with his mouth watering, Rube followed his nose.

Before long, he heard talking and laughter coming faintly from somewhere up ahead. He turned a corner into an open plaza and the sounds suddenly became much louder. He scanned the area and immediately pinpointed where the noise was coming from: at the opposite side of the square was a large building with a series of columns along its face. Between the columns many people moved about.

He walked over to it. As he entered between two of the

towering columns, he saw that it was some sort of giant banquet hall. Aromas from a wide variety of cuisines engulfed him from all sides, making him practically drool. Assorted food vendors lined the sides, whilst the central area was filled with people lounging around low tables, reclining on cushions. The tables were laden with food—more than they could all possibly eat. Everybody was stuffing their faces. Juices dribbled down their chins. Greasy smears adorned their clothing. And everybody was fat. Very fat.

Rube took this in with horrified fascination. Then his stomach grumbled loudly—not that anyone could hear it over the din. He sidled up to a nearby table, eyeing up its occupants. One man lay flat on his back, snoring. Good. Rube leant cautiously over him and reached his hand out towards a juicy chicken drumstick. He waited until the other people sitting at the table weren't looking then grabbed the succulent morsel. It instantly vanished into thin air. Nobody noticed. He ate it hungrily and licked his fingers clean. Surreptitiously dropping the bones on top of some others, he helped himself to a piece of pork crackling and popped it into his mouth. Mmm, delicious. He closed his eyes momentarily, savouring it as he chewed. It stuck to his teeth a bit. Were there any toothpicks? He scanned the table. Nope, none there.

He worked his way carefully over to the next table to see if they had any. Oh yes, there they were. He waited until no one was looking and secured one. And while he was at it, why not sneak that delicious-looking piece of chocolate cake?

"Eeeek!" A woman's scream pierced the air. Rube almost dropped the piece of cake in fright. She was right next to him. He looked around to see what might have caused the commotion.

"What's wrong, Mavis?" the man next to her asked.

Mavis pointed a shaking finger at the rest of the chocolate cake sitting in the centre of the table. "Tha … that cake just disappeared." Mavis's three chins wobbled as much as her voice shook.

"Don't be silly. It's right there. You're pointing at it." The man stated matter-of-factly. He belched.

"No. I mean, a piece of it. I was eyeing it up, you see, and then … it just disappeared." She started to heave herself upright.

Rube stepped quickly backwards. Time to make himself scarce. He turned on his heel and wove his way out between the tables. He glanced back over his shoulder. The woman Mavis was still on the floor, trying to stand. Rube grinned to himself and took a bite of cake. Then he pilfered a small bunch of grapes and stepped out into the weak sunlight.

That had hit the spot. But now he was thirsty. He walked over to the well in the centre of the plaza. He glanced around him. Could he risk it? Nobody was around—all too busy eating, presumably. He stared at the well. Should he make the whole thing invisible? Just the bucket and rope? Or none of it? He squinted back at the food hall. He couldn't tell if anyone was watching. It was too risky. He shook his head and walked briskly out of the plaza.

The alleyway he had chosen to exit by was narrow. A large shape entered the other end. An extremely fat man. Rube pressed himself flat against the wall. But as the man approached, he realised that there was not enough room for both of them. Rube spun on his heel and walked quickly back out the way he had come and waited in the plaza. The man soon lumbered past, headed straight towards the food hall. Was everyone here fat? Did *Gula* have something to do with eating too much?

He re-entered the alleyway. A few blocks away, he came to another, smaller square. This one had a fountain playing in the centre of it. Aha! Satisfied that nobody was around, he walked to the fountain and gratefully opened his mouth under one of the jets of water. Mmm, bliss. His thirst quenched, he plunged his hands into the water at the base of the fountain, washing off the grease and dust. He rubbed them over his face and hair. That was better. Now, time to find that last gate.

Chapter 24

IN SEARCH OF HONEY

It was mid-morning. The sun was already high in the bright blue sky. Another beautiful day in Tyrelia. They had spent the night at the edge of a meadow nestled in a hollowed-out section of the cliff. After a breakfast of bread, cheese and salami, washed down by refreshing water, they'd discovered a bush laden with juicy, ripe blackberries. They'd picked the bush clean.

For the past couple of hours, they had been working their way along the grassy plateau, which sloped gently up towards the towering mountain.

"Aha," Willow announced. She was bending down, peering at something on the ground.

"What is it?" Freya asked. She crouched beside Willow. "Is it something to eat? Has the Ancient provided?"

Willow snorted. She pointed at the small, black pebble-sized object nestled amongst the blades of grass. "That, Freya, is sheep dung. So, no, we are not going to eat it," she said, grinning.

Freya blushed bright red. "I knew that."

Willow stood and strode off, looking intently at the ground as she went. "Here's more. And there," she said, pointing.

Freya caught up. "Yep, and there's a whole lot of flattened grass over there."

"I reckon the flock spent the night in this area. They're not far off."

They set off once more.

Baa, baa.

"Did you hear that?" Freya asked.

"Sure did." Willow quickened her pace.

There! A sheep. And another.

Willow scanned from side to side. She spotted a large boulder. A cap, like her own, floated above it. She turned to Freya, touching her finger to her lips, her eyes mischievous. "Shhh."

Freya nodded. They crept towards the boulder. A strange rattling sound was coming from it. Snoring.

Willow sneaked up behind the boulder, then, snaking out a hand, knocked the cap off her brother's head. "Wake up, sleepy head," she yelled.

Alex yelped and scrambled to his feet, his eyes wide, disoriented. Then he spotted Willow.

"It's you," he exclaimed. In a single, fluid motion, he leapt over the boulder and tackled his twin.

They both went down in a tangle of lanky limbs. Willow shrieked then started laughing hysterically as Alex tickled her, pinning her to the ground.

"Stop. Stop. I'm sorry!"

"So you should be, giving me a fright like that."

Freya couldn't help it. She giggled.

Alex froze at the sound, then looked up. Seeing Freya, he scrambled off his sister and stood up. "Who are you?" he demanded, scowling.

"Alex, Alex. Calm down. This is my friend Freya." Willow rolled to her knees, gesturing towards Freya. "And Freya, this is Alex."

Alex grunted and nodded, still looking suspiciously at Freya. "What's she doing here?"

Willow got to her feet and brushed grass off herself. She took a deep breath. "Well, that's a bit of a long story. So how about we all sit down, and Freya can tell you herself."

~

When she had finished recounting her adventures to Alex, and how the clues that the tablet had revealed had led them to this place, he gave a low whistle.

"Wow," he said, staring at Freya in admiration, shaking his head. "That is some story. What's the latest clue, again?"

Freya chanted:

"Go up Helix River, to its source
At the waterfall—a powerful force—
Follow the sounds of birds up high
Of honey bees buzzing as they fly

When sunlight fades to shades of grey
At dusk watch for nature's display
From whence the cloud comes, will reveal
The path which is elsewise concealed

"The next thing we need to do is find honey, up near the waterfall. Do you know it?" Freya asked hopefully.

Alex nodded, grinning. The same grin as Willow's. "Yeah, I know the waterfall. It's only a couple of hours from here. Let's go there now," he exclaimed.

Freya and Willow nodded eagerly.

~

At first it was just a faint rumble. Then, as they got closer, the sound grew louder and louder. Half an hour ago, the meadow had given way to a pine forest. Now the ground rose steeply underfoot. It was littered with dry pine needles, pine cones and small rocks which crunched softly as they walked.

Freya made out a darker shape up ahead. "What's that?" she asked, pointing.

Alex glanced back over his shoulder to see what she was referring to. "Rock," he said.

Sure enough, they had arrived at a tumble of boulders at the base of a cliff.

"Now what?" Freya asked.

Willow grinned as she followed her brother, who was already scrambling up onto the first rock. "Now we climb," she said.

It wasn't as hard as it looked. The boulders were big but smooth. Using both hands, and poking her toe into a crevice, Freya clambered up on to the first big boulder. Up and over, up and over they went, keeping as close to the cliff face as possible, careful not to slip into the big gaps between the rocks.

After several minutes, they arrived at the top of the rockfall. As she stood beside Alex and Willow and finally looked up, Freya gasped. Fifty metres ahead of them towered a sheer cliff. She craned her neck to gaze upwards. From the very top, water poured over the lip and cascaded down the face in a froth of white until it plunged many metres below them into a pool in the canyon below. The sound was deafening. Fine droplets of water misted on their hair and faces: they had found the waterfall.

She stood mesmerised for a few moments, before turning to

Alex, and, to be heard above the thunder of the waterfall, yelled, "So, where are the bees?"

Alex shrugged. "I don't know."

"What do you mean you don't know? You said you did!" Freya accused.

"I said I knew where the waterfall was," he shouted.

"Your tablet," Willow intervened. "What else did it say—the part after the waterfall?"

"Oh yeah. Umm … *Follow the sounds of the birds up high, Of honey bees buzzing as they fly*," Freya quoted.

Willow craned her neck as she carefully spun on the boulder and scanned the cliff beside them. "Oooh, look," she exclaimed, pointing.

Alex and Freya looked up. There, circling high above the top of the cliff, were two eagles. She could just discern their cries faintly above the thunder of the falls.

"Okay, so there's the birds. Where are the bees then?"

"It says to follow the sounds of the birds," Willow said. She started leaping from boulder to boulder towards the cliff. Alex followed suit. When Willow reached the base of the cliff, she worked her way along towards the waterfall, inspecting and feeling the surface closely as she went. She found some footholds as she started climbing up the face but didn't get far before she jumped back down.

Meanwhile, Alex continued past the spot where Willow was climbing, scanning the cliff face as he went. "Hey, I think I've found something," he cried.

"What is it?" Freya asked. She leapt from boulder to boulder towards him. But when she arrived at the spot where she'd last seen him, he had vanished. "Where are you?" she called.

"I'm in here." His voice echoed oddly.

It wasn't until she was directly opposite it, that she saw it. Alex was standing in a cave. No, it wasn't a cave. As she stepped into it, she gazed upwards. It was a crevice. The thunder of the waterfall faded and now a constant buzzing filled the air. High above them was an enormous, dark, fuzzy mass. Little black dots darted all around it. Bees.

Chapter 25

IN SEARCH OF THE CAVE PEOPLE

Saff swiped at a low-hanging branch in frustration. It flicked back and struck him on his face.

"Ouch! That hurt," he barked, rubbing his cheek.

"Are you all right?" Thyst asked. She was following behind him and could only see his back.

Saff sighed. "It's just that we've been wandering around in this wretched forest for days now. And still no sign of those Cave People."

"Tell me again, what did Freya say about them?"

"Well, that they're small. She said that the adults were the size of children. They spoke in a guttural language—only the chief spoke a little bit of our language. And that they melted into the forest. They could be watching us right now for all we know."

Thyst twisted around on her saddle and peered intently into the foliage around them. "I see eyes," she whispered.

"Where?" Saff turned in his saddle to see where she was

looking and squinted into the trees.

"There." Thyst pointed.

Suddenly, a squirrel leapt from the branch she had been pointing out, chattering loudly as it went.

Thyst squawked, clutching at her chest. "That gave me a fright."

Saff snorted as he turned back around and urged his horse forward once more.

"Are you laughing at me?" Thyst demanded, her cheeks colouring.

"Me? No, of course not," Saff smirked.

Thyst took a deep breath to calm her racing heart. "Anything else about the Cave People?"

Saff's back stiffened. He twisted back to Thyst. "Actually, yes. I remember now. She talked about the caves being behind a waterfall. So, we need to find a river." He flashed a grin at Thyst.

He really did have a lovely smile. And the way those amazing blue eyes sparkled, his mouth framed by that black beard ... Thyst shook her head, as if to shake the unwanted thoughts out, and urged Dapple to follow Thunder. Her cheeks burned bright red. What in the Land was she thinking?

They worked their way eastwards, roughly parallel to the Chasm. Every ten minutes or so, they headed back to the Chasm.

"See anything yet?" Thyst asked, as she stepped up beside Saff. "Oh!" The sight of Tyrelia took her breath away every time.

Saff glanced at her, then turned quickly away, frowning at the Wall across the Chasm. "I guess I still don't believe in the Ancient, then. If indeed that is the reason why I can't see Tyrelia."

Thyst patted his arm, sympathy in her eyes. She sighed. "I don't know. I hope Rube manages to figure something out."

Saff swallowed hard, his larynx bobbing in his throat. "Mmm. I still don't understand how all knowledge of the Ancient could've been lost."

Thyst flicked her eyes to him. "A thousand years is a long time for information to be passed on from Watcher to Watcher. And all that time, nobody could enter Tyrelia. Watchers were relentlessly pursued by the Master's Guards. They burnt all the records." She shrugged. "I can see how it could happen."

Saff sighed. "I suppose so. C'mon, let's keep going."

Thyst swept her gaze greedily across the horizon, from the far right to the far left. "Oh my goodness," she exclaimed.

"What?"

"There. There." She pointed emphatically at the Wall somewhere well off to their left.

Saff shook his head despairingly. "You're going to have to tell me what you can see, Thyst."

"It's an archway, Saff! Like the one Freya described on the other side of Medar, near Andor. Do you know what I think?" She turned to Saff, her long brown curls bouncing around her face, her violet eyes as big as her smile was wide.

Saff grinned at her.

"The old bridge!" they both exclaimed together.

~

Fifteen minutes later, they emerged on the banks of a river, the thunderous roar of the water cascading into the Chasm filling the air.

Saff had to raise his voice to be heard above the tumult. "Can you see the archway, Thyst?"

"Yes," she shouted. "It's right opposite." Reflexively, she pointed, then quickly dropped her arm. "Sorry," she mumbled.

Saff walked towards the Chasm and stood as close to the edge as he dared. He leaned out and peered downwards.

"Can you see anything?" Thyst called.

He shook his head, then dropped to his hands and knees, then onto his belly. Slithering forward, he peered once more over the edge. After what seemed an age, he slithered backwards and stood up, wiping droplets off his face with his sleeve. "I think I can see something. It's kinda hard. There's so much mist, I can't really be sure. No idea how to get down there, though." His voice was muffled as he wiped his sleeve back and forth over his face and beard. He dropped his arm, took a step towards Thyst, then suddenly froze, staring at a spot behind her.

She spun around and squeaked with fright, stumbling backwards. Clutching at her chest, she stared at the small person who had noiselessly materialised behind her. He only came up to just above her waist. His skin was darker than hers and, had she not known better, she would've mistaken him for a boy, not a fully-grown man. He was dressed in animal skins and furs and held a long, sharp wooden spear. It was pointed at her chest.

Saff strode quickly to her side. "Hello, friend," he said in a cordial tone to the small man. He held his hands out, palms upturned, showing that he wasn't armed.

The man made a guttural noise and thrust his spear closer towards Thyst.

She took a step backwards, also holding her hands out, palms up. "We're friends of Freya," she blurted.

The man's eyes went wide. "Freya," he repeated. He immediately withdrew his spear and, cupping his hands to his mouth, made a bird call.

Immediately, five, six, seven other small men stepped out from the trees around them. But their eyes were friendly. One of them gestured towards the waterfall and beckoned. "Freya,

Freya," he said, smiling.

Saff and Thyst raised their eyebrows at each other, smiling in relief. They'd found the Cave People.

Chapter 26

LEVEL SEVEN

The gate to Level Seven loomed before him. A C E D I A. Rube found a low wall nearby. He sat down to rest and mop his brow, wondering about this level's word.

He gazed out at the view: from this high, he could see a great distance. The gates from each level aligned exactly one below the other. Way below him, at the base of the city, a perfectly straight road headed out like an arrow towards Targa. At the other end of the road, Targa looked like a toy town made of a child's building blocks.

He marvelled at the tiny carts drawn by miniature horses making their way along the road. On either side of the road, the neatly tended fields resembled a patchwork quilt spread around the city in various shades of brown, green and yellow. He could just make out the workers in the fields. He wondered which ones were Martha and Jack. He sighed. They were the reason he was here. Them and Thomas … and all the inhabitants of the Golden City. If his hunch was right, maybe he could free them all?

He straightened his back and turned to study the gate. All the other gateways had been constructed of normal, grey stone. This one was black. Ominous. Brooding. He shivered.

At that moment, he heard the thunder of hooves pounding and the rattle of carriage wheels on the road. He whipped his head around, trying to determine which direction the sound was coming from.

Suddenly, four splendidly attired Guards came galloping out through the Level Seven gate, followed closely by two magnificent black destriers pulling an ornate black carriage. Four more mounted Guards brought up the rear.

They galloped so close past Rube that his cloak flapped and his hair lifted off his forehead. Rube gripped the edge of the wall tightly as they passed. A stab of fear shot through him, just looking at the carriage. But as soon as it passed, so too did the feeling.

He waited a minute, straining his ears, just to make sure that nobody else was going to gallop out and trample him. All clear.

He stood up, massaged his hip, then walked over to the archway. He took a deep breath to calm his racing heart. This was it. Now or never. He stepped through the entrance … and nothing. He wasn't dead. He smiled wryly to himself. Now, where would the Master's library be?

He looked around, then set off along the main road, presumably towards the Master's palace. If he survived this, he'd have a few stories to tell.

There was no doubt about it, the buildings were beautiful, the grass verges immaculately trimmed, not a speck of litter to be seen. But it was so quiet. An elderly man shuffled along the footpath on the opposite side of the street. Just up ahead, an old woman sat in a rocking chair outside her house, beside her front door. She looked sad, worn out, Rube noted, as he approached.

"Who's there?" she croaked, cocking her head, listening

intently. She was blind.

Rube froze and tried to breathe quietly.

"Is that you, Alfred?" she asked.

Rube stepped carefully onto the grass verge then crossed to the other side of the road. A weak ray of sunlight broke through the cloud pall overhead. Up ahead, something glinted. As he drew nearer, Rube saw a high wrought-iron rail fence with spikes all along the top. Behind the fence manicured lawns and sculptured gardens stretched as far as the eye could see. And off in the distance rose a magnificent palace, all turrets and towers. The weak sun sparkled off gold-plated domes that adorned the roof. The Master's residence.

Stern-looking Guards stood either side of the gates, which were shut tight. There was no way Rube would be entering the palace grounds until those gates opened. He might be invisible, but that didn't make him insubstantial: the spacings between the railings were too narrow, and the fence too high for him to climb, especially now with his injury. He shook his head in exasperation, and headed to the right, following along the wrought-iron fence. Maybe there was another gate, somewhere else?

He walked and walked. The day wore on. Although the houses on the street opposite were beautiful, there was little evidence of life. He saw only old people every now and then, shuffling along the street on some errand. And it was eerily quiet.

After an hour, he stopped to rest and eat some lunch. He found a bench seat in a deserted park and dug out some bread, ham and cheese that Leena had given him. Some crumbs fell as he ate and, before long, a pigeon swooped down to gobble them up. Before he knew it, three more pigeons turned up and pecked hopefully around his feet. This would never do! They would give him away.

"Shoo," he hissed. The pigeons strutted around but didn't leave. An elderly woman wandered into the park and glanced at the pigeons curiously. Rube got up and hurried away, causing the pigeons to scatter in a flurry of wings.

He continued walking adjacent to the perimeter fence, finishing off his bread as he went. Another hour passed. He stopped to rest, leaning against the fence, massaging his hip. The cloud had lowered and now a light mist swirled in the air. He pushed himself upright and continued on his way.

The cloud became denser, and before long he was walking through fog. He couldn't see more than a metre ahead. He trailed his hand along the palings but maintained his invisibility. He wasn't about to make the same mistake that the other Watchers had near Andoria!

So intent was he on peering ahead into the fog, that he nearly missed the gate. If he hadn't been feeling the fence, he surely would have. The doubling up of palings either side of the gate gave him pause and, sure enough, upon closer inspection, there was a latch. Holding his breath, he slipped his hand between two bars and tried to work the mechanism. With a *click* the gate swung inwards.

He was in!

Chapter 27

IN THE MASTER'S MANSION

Closing the gate quietly behind him, Rube shuffled along the path through the thick fog. He could see grass only a metre either side of the path. He still couldn't believe that he'd been able to enter so easily.

After what seemed an age, but was probably only fifteen minutes or so, he made out a darker shape ahead of him. A brighter square patch glowed within it and became more and more solid until the palace building materialised just metres in front of him. The brighter square patch was a window next to a closed door. Judging by the well off to his left, the wooden buckets standing beside the back door and the delicious smells emanating from the building, he'd arrived at the kitchens.

Now, how to get inside?

He sidled up to the building and peered into the window. Yes, it was a kitchen: the large room had flagstone floors, whitewashed walls, and timber trusses overhead. An assortment of pots and pans hung from the rafters, alongside bunches of onions and garlic. One wall boasted a fireplace in the centre with a fire burning brightly. A flagstone hearth ran the length of the wall. Various benches, cupboards and tables lined the other walls. An elderly woman stood at a large table in the middle of the room, flour up to her elbows as she kneaded a mound of dough. She wore a mob cap to hold back her hair, but grey tendrils escaped and clung to her brow.

Over on the stove, a pot of stew bubbled away. The aroma wafted through the cracks around the door. Rube's stomach grumbled without warning.

"Hello?" the old woman stopped her kneading and jerked her head up, listening. "Winston? Is that you?"

Suddenly, from not too far away, some dogs started barking. Rube jumped and stepped away from the window. He pressed himself against the wall between the window and the door and peered out into the foggy whiteness.

Shortly, he discerned the stomping of boots accompanied by a vague dark shape approaching. Just a metre from Rube, the man veered off to the other side of the door. The barking resolved into whimpers and snuffles, accompanied by the man murmuring, "How's my boys? Did you miss me? Did you miss me?" Then he stomped towards the door once more.

He levered his boots off and set them neatly side by side before opening the door wide. "Hello, Peggy my love!" he exclaimed, stepping quickly inside and catching the woman in a big embrace.

She giggled and flapped at him with her floury hand. "Stop it, stop it. I'm covered in flour. And you've left the door wide open," she scolded.

Winston strode back to the door and closed it smartly, before walking over to the stew and inspecting the contents of the pot.

He grabbed the ladle and stirred the mixture before scooping a portion out. He blew on it, then ate it.

"Winston!" Peggy scolded again. "The Master will be right furious, he will. Move along now, go and clean up."

"All right," Winston grumbled. "Don't bite my head off."

Rube had sneaked inside behind Winston and stood beside the roaring fire. He was damp through from the fog and had started to shiver. He held his hands out and soaked up the warmth whilst the two old people hugged and scolded each other. Very sweet. He thought wistfully about Isabella, his own dear wife, dead these past fourteen years. How nice it would've been to be growing old with her now.

"Winston … ?" Peggy's voice wavered uncertainly from behind him.

Rube glanced around at her, and with horror saw that she was staring straight at him, pointing with a shaking finger. He looked down at himself and understood the source of her angst: gentle tendrils of steam rose off him as his robes dried out. Off his head, his shoulders, his arms and his back. The whole steamy outline of a person.

Rube quickly stepped past the fire towards the inner door, that led deeper into the house, leaving a wispy trail of steam behind him.

"What is it?" Winston called from the hallway.

"Winston, can you come in here please?" Peggy tremored. Her voice went up sharply at the end.

Winston poked his head around the door frame. Seeing his wife's white face and staring eyes, he looked in the direction she was pointing, which was somewhere in between where Rube had been, and where he was now.

"A ghost," she whispered.

"Err," Winston said, stepping into the room, "I can't see anything."

"There was an outline of a man. Right *there*." She pointed. "And then he moved. *There*."

Winston walked slowly to where she was pointing, waving his hands in front of him, trying to capture the ghost. To no avail. Rube was already safely out of the kitchen and walking quietly down the hallway.

"There doesn't seem to be anything here …" he heard as he left.

Rube passed a washroom, one closed door, another closed door. He stopped and listened. Nothing. Cautiously, he opened the door.

A short hallway stretched before him ending at a pair of beautiful, gilded doors. He wiped his clammy hands on his robes and took a deep breath. He strode to the doors. Frosted-glass panes adorned them, decorated with palm trees and peacocks. Rube peered through, with his hand on the gilded handle. The coast was clear.

He quietly opened the door and slipped into the grand dining room. He gazed around in awe. A long, polished mahogany table stretched the entire length of the room. Ornate chandeliers dangled at intervals from the ceiling. Massive mirrors alternating with giant paintings adorned the wall to his right, whilst the left-hand wall boasted enormous glass windows framed by deep red velvet drapes. An intricate parquet floor gleamed underfoot.

He didn't linger to admire the paintings but scuttled the length of the room to matching frosted-glass and gilded doors at the far end. He peeked through the glass before opening the door just wide enough to slip through.

He was in a drawing room. Here, various groupings of dark brown leather couches surrounded occasional tables. A bar of sorts was to his right against the wall at this end of the room. A billiard table took pride of place in the centre of the space. Over to his left was a card table. Again, windows ran the length of the room on his left, while the right-hand wall displayed some tapestries and more paintings. A plush carpet cushioned his feet. He was momentarily tempted to help himself to a small glass of brandy, then decided against the idea.

He hurried on through the room, weaving his way around the billiard table and between the scattered couches. At the other end, he paused briefly, listening at the door before opening it and slipping through.

He was in the main entrance foyer. A grand staircase arrested his attention. It swept up to the second floor. The ceiling soared overhead into a dome above the staircase. The marble floor alternated white and black tiles, reminding him of a giant chessboard. He glanced around. A series of doors led off the space at intervals. Another wing headed off directly opposite where he'd entered the foyer. The main entrance doors were to his left. He scanned the area once more, before nodding briefly to himself and heading up the stairs.

At the top of the stairs he paused. Should he go left or right? He gazed up at the painting that adorned the wall in front of him. It was of the Master: a dark figure with swirling robes, standing triumphantly on a pile of rocks. He leaned in to have a closer look. No, not rocks. People. Masses of writhing people. Ugh. He stepped back. The painted figure held a gleaming sword aloft, pointing to the left. Okay, left it was.

He set off down the carpeted hallway. The first few doors he came to were open. He glanced into the rooms as he passed. A powder room. A bedroom. The next door was shut. Should he open it? Maybe he'd come back if he couldn't find the library. He kept going. Massive, solid oak doors marked the end of the hallway ahead of him. His heart started beating a little faster. He picked up his pace.

He could smell them before he reached the doorway. Books. Beautiful parchment. He wiped his hands once more on his robes. He listened at the closed door before placing his hand on the large, round brass knob. He turned it slowly. The door swung soundlessly open. He smiled. He had found it. The Master's library.

Chapter 28

THE BROKEN BRIDGE

After clambering down the cliff face, following the small Cave dwellers, Saff and Thyst were ushered into a large cave. Using hand-gestures, they were told to stay put. They stared around. It was just as Freya had described: a large fire, with rocks around the perimeter and cooking stones set up over it, smouldered near the mouth of the cavern. Sticks and dry moss were piled against the far wall—fuel for the fire. A couple of small women sat tending the fire and cooking food. Not too far away, some more women thumped away with mortars and pestles. The little people's skin was deeper-toned, and they dressed in furs. Overhead, all sorts of dried herbs and meats hung in bunches from a series of fibrous ropes strung across the ceiling.

Shortly, two of the huntsmen came back. Beckoning for Saff and Thyst to follow them, they guided them out of the cave, along a wide path with a low rock wall constructed along its outside edge. The Chasm dropped away immediately below the wall. Across the other side of the Chasm rose a rocky, vertical cliff. Thyst craned her neck, gazing up to the top of the cliff opposite. They were too deep within the Chasm to see Tyrelia.

Disappointed, she dropped her eyes back to the small huntsman she was following.

He trotted along the dusty path, then up a flight of stairs. Thyst, Saff and the second huntsman followed in single file. At the top of the stairs, two guards with long wooden spears stood on a landing, either side of a generous cave entrance. At their approach, the guards crossed their spears over the opening, barring their entry. The lead huntsman approached the guards and spoke to them, gesturing behind him at the two Watchers. The guards' eyes flicked to them, then they snapped to attention, pulled their spears upright and thumped the spear butts in unison on the platform. The huntsman led the way into a spacious cave, beckoning them to follow.

Thyst blinked a few times, waiting for her eyes to adjust to the dim interior. In the centre of the cave, a few metres in front of her, rose a grand stone throne atop a plinth with a flight of stairs hewn into the front. It appeared to grow out of the cave floor. Perched on the throne was a diminutive man wrapped in an animal skin cloak. A wolf's muzzle protruded above his face. The animal's long, yellow fangs framed his forehead and cast his face into shadow. He held an intricately carved staff in one hand. Thyst stared at him in awe. Then something poked her in the back. Saff, who was standing to her right, tugged on her sleeve. Out of the corner of her eye, she saw movement and immediately dropped to her knees, as the others had already done. She peered out from under her lashes at the huntsman to her left, wondering what the protocol was. It was clear that they had been brought into the presence of the clan chief.

The chief issued a command and the huntsmen stood. Thyst and Saff mirrored them. The chief stared at them.

Saff cleared his throat. "Sir," he said, "I'm Saff and this is

Thyst. We're friends of Freya's."

The chief leaned forward slightly. "Mph. Freya." He nodded. Then he pointed at Saff. "Saff," he said. Then, after a brief pause, "Watcher Saff?"

"Yes!" Saff confirmed, surprised. "I'm Watcher Saff, and this is Watcher Thyst," he motioned to his left.

Thyst bowed her head.

"We were wondering if you could help us …" Saff started.

The chief shook his head. He said something in his language.

"Oh," Saff said. He glanced at Thyst.

She shrugged.

"Umm …" Saff tried again. "Do you know Tyrelia?"

The chief's eyes lit up with understanding. "Uh," he nodded. "Tyrelia." He pointed up through the ceiling of the cave towards where the top of the opposite cliff of the Chasm would be.

"Can you help us get there?" Thyst blurted.

The chief frowned at her and shook his head slightly with incomprehension.

"We," Saff gestured to himself and Thyst, "want to go to Tyrelia." Saff pointed in the same direction the chief had.

The chief stared at him intently for a moment, before slapping his free hand on his leg, throwing his head back and roaring with laughter. The two huntsmen stared at their chief, startled, then at the two Watchers, their eyes full of questions.

"What are we going to do?" Thyst whispered to Saff.

Saff cleared his throat, holding his hands palm-up in front of him.

Suddenly, the chief stopped laughing and issued a series of commands to the huntsmen. They snapped to attention, then one tugged at Thyst's sleeve, urging her to head back towards the cave entrance. She followed him obediently.

They went back down the flight of stairs, but instead of returning along the same path that they'd come on, the huntsman turned the other way and headed downwards, deeper into the Chasm.

Thyst became aware of a dull roar that had been in the background since they had arrived. A mist of fine droplets swirled in the air, settling on her hair and face. Above, she made out other paths, zig-zagging their way to the top of the cliff, a long way above them. Judging by the lightness of the sky, she guessed it was late afternoon.

As the huntsman led the way along the path, Thyst stuck close to the rocky cliff wall rising almost vertically beside them, running her hand along the rough surface. They came to a stairway hewn into the cliff face ascending to the next level, but continued past it, walking right under the waterfall. It was like entering a cocoon, the rock wall forming one side and a cascading curtain of water the other, shielding the Chasm from her view and making her feel strangely safe.

Emerging from the other side of the waterfall, a faintly nasty but familiar odour hit her nostrils. Ablutions. The huntsman continued straight past this cave then stopped at a low wall blocking the path. He carefully climbed over it then gestured to the others to follow.

"Freya told me about this," Saff called to Thyst over the thunder of the falls. "They're taking us to the broken bridge."

Thyst grinned at Saff. "That's good … isn't it?"

He nodded, smiling, his blue eyes sparkling.

The path continued for a short way before leading to some more stairs going down the cliff face. As they descended, the light grew weaker, but still the stair wound down and down until it was hard to see where they were going. There were no caves, just stairs and landings, zig-zagging down the face of the cliff. Eventually, they came to a larger landing that jutted out into the Chasm.

The lead huntsman stopped to one side and gestured for Thyst and Saff to look. They peered into the gloom. The landing had handrails on either side.

"By the Master, the bridge!" Saff breathed. He cautiously walked out, one hand resting on the rail.

Thyst followed on the other side. She had gone only ten paces when she saw that the bridge ended: it had apparently simply fallen away.

Beside her, Saff dropped to his hands and knees and crawled to the edge. Below, there was nothing but blackness.

"What do you see?" Thyst yelled.

Saff screwed up his eyes, squinting into the gloom. "The other side of the broken bridge. I reckon it's about twenty metres that's missing."

"Oh," Thyst said, her shoulders sagging. "That's not good."

Saff crawled back from the edge, before standing up and brushing his hands together. "No, it's not," he agreed, "but I think it can be rebuilt." He grinned at Thyst.

She shook her head, incredulous, her brown curls bouncing around her face. "You're joking."

"No," Saff said, placing his hands on her shoulders. "I'm completely serious."

Chapter 29

THE HONEY CLUE

Freya frowned. "How are we going to climb all the way up there?"

"Hey, where are you?" Willow's voice came faintly from outside.

Freya stepped back out of the crevice and scrambled onto a boulder. "In here, Willow," she called, beckoning. "Come and see."

Alex had started climbing the crevice, finding tenuous fingerholds and pulling his lean frame up with strong arms, whilst wedging his toes into tiny gaps. He climbed higher and higher.

Willow joined Freya and stood beside her, watching her twin. "Be careful, Alex," she murmured.

Alex disappeared into gloom. All they could hear was the droning of the bees and the faint thunder of the waterfall outside. They waited anxiously a few moments. Freya nibbled at a fingernail.

"There!" Willow said, grabbing Freya's arm, pointing.

Alex was returning. Slowly, carefully, he worked his way

back down to the base of the crevice.

"Well?" Willow demanded, as soon as he jumped safely back beside them.

Alex brushed dust off his hands. "I couldn't get close enough," he said, shaking his head. Too many bees buzzing around. Look." He held out his hand. There was an angry red swelling at the base of his thumb. "I got stung."

Willow took her brother's hand and, positioning her nail carefully at the base of the sting still protruding out of his palm, scraped it out and flicked it away. "You okay?" she asked.

"Thanks," he said, blowing on his hand. "Yeah, I will be. We're going to have to smoke 'em out."

"Smoke?" Freya asked, bewildered.

Willow nodded. "Yes, of course. Smoke makes bees sleepy," she explained.

Alex was already outside, jumping down the boulders, back towards the trees. "We'll need to make a fire inside the crevice," he yelled back over his shoulder. "Come on, help me collect some pine cones."

They gathered as many pine cones as they could and grabbed several green branches and took them back to the cliff. They piled the kindling within the mouth of the crevice, far below the massive hive.

Alex felt about in his pocket, then suddenly looked stricken. "I've left my flint behind. It's back with the sheep," he moaned.

Freya swung her satchel around to her front. "Don't worry. I've got my tinder box," she said. She pulled it out and, kneeling beside their pile of pine cones and dry twigs, she struck a spark onto the kindling. It fizzled out. "Come on," she breathed. She struck her flint again. This time the spark caught. Freya blew on it gently and, before long, a fire was blazing.

"Good job," Alex said, his voice full of admiration.

Freya blushed. "Thanks," she said.

Alex tied a piece of rope to a sturdy stick. He slung it over his shoulder. "Right, up I go. Wait until I climb high enough before you make it smoky."

He started climbing. After a few minutes, they couldn't see him anymore.

"How's it going?" Willow called up.

"Not yet," the response floated back down to them.

They waited a few more minutes.

"Okay," Alex bellowed from above. "Start making smoke!"

Willow placed one of the green branches on top of the crackling flames. Immediately, thick smoke billowed up.

Freya coughed and her eyes watered.

"How's that?" Willow shouted.

"More!"

Willow threw two more green branches on the fire, while Freya fanned it with another. Now both Freya and Willow were coughing uncontrollably, their eyes streaming.

A thumping sound came from overhead. A few dead bees tumbled into the green boughs covering the fire. More thumping followed by a triumphant yelp from Alex.

A lump of bee hive came hurtling through the billowing smoke and landed with a *whump* on the branches. The fire hissed and sputtered.

"Quick, Freya, grab it!" Willow urged.

Freya snatched a branch and prodded the comb until it slid off the other side. She ran around and picked it up.

"Ouch! That's hot," she yelped, dropping it to suck her burnt fingers.

"Use your shield."

Freya shrugged off her shield and scooped up the section of honey comb. She ran out of the fissure and tipped it onto the nearest boulder, gasping for air.

Willow was right behind her.

Freya reached around and pulled her tablet out of her satchel and whipped off the cover. "Okay, can you drip honey on it?"

Willow picked up the cooling lump of hive. It was sticky and covered with bodies of bees. She held it over the tablet and slowly, slowly, honey oozed out, dripping onto the surface.

Freya spread the warm substance around with her index finger. Her heart started beating faster as silvery writing, faint at first, appeared under the golden smear.

"Thanks for waiting for me." Alex had come up behind them. His face was streaked with soot.

"Look, Alex," Willow said, without turning.

He leant over Freya's shoulder. "By the Ancient!" he said in wonder. "What does it say?"

Freya wiped the surface so that the honey was smeared very thinly. She cleared her throat and read out:

Deep within the mountain rift
Find the hermit to claim your gift
He will guide you in your task
You won't receive if you don't ask

Alex whistled between his teeth. "A hermit," he said.

"A gift," Willow exclaimed.

"A task?" Freya asked.

They all looked at each other and burst out laughing.

"So, now what?" Alex asked, when they'd caught their breaths.

"Well," Freya said, "I need to find *the mountain rift*."

"Do you think it's that crevice where the bees are?"

Freya sucked the honey off her burnt fingers, frowning. "I suppose we should look," she said.

They made their way back to the crevice. The fire was still smouldering, and smoke clogged the air.

Fanning her hand in front of her nose, Willow stepped past the fire towards the back of the crevice. "It's not very deep," she called. "I can't go any further than this." She came back out.

"Here, let me look." Freya squeezed past Willow. She didn't spend long in the crevice before she too, came back out. "You're right. There's nothing there."

"So," Alex said slowly, "there must be another rift then?" He gazed around them. Up towards the eagles circling above, then to the top of the waterfall and across to the other side of the valley. "It could be anywhere!"

Willow had climbed on a boulder and sat there, frowning. Suddenly, she slapped her thigh. "That's it!"

"What?" Freya and Alex asked at the same time, turning to her.

"The part of the poem after the bit about the honey bees," she said. And she quoted:

"When sunlight fades to shades of grey
At dusk watch for nature's display
From whence the cloud comes, will reveal
The path which is elsewise concealed."

"Yes! You got it, Willow," Freya said. "Except I don't know what 'whence' means."

"It's old language for 'where'," Willow explained.

"How do you know that?" Freya asked.

"Well, it can be a.bit boring watching sheep. I read an awful lot." Willow shrugged her shoulders dismissively.

Alex chipped in. "What do you suppose 'nature's display' is?"

"The next line talks about a cloud. Maybe it's a magnificent sunset display with cool cloud shapes?" Willow surmised, sweeping her hand overhead.

They all looked up at the sky. Not a cloud in sight.

"Maybe a cloud forms at sunset?" Freya suggested hopefully.

"Well, there's only one way to find out. Wait for dusk," Alex said.

They all grinned at each other. Then slowly, Alex's grin faded.

"What's wrong?" Willow asked.

"I can't stay," Alex said dejectedly. "I've got to go back to the sheep."

"Oh," Freya said. "That's a shame. Are you sure? What if we need you again? You were so good with the honey."

This time, Alex blushed. "Well," he cleared his throat, "er … you and Willow have done fine without me up until now. I'm sure you'll do just fine this time. Besides, I can come back in the morning. I can't wait to hear what you discover."

Freya twirled her braid in her fingers. "Great. We'll see you tomorrow then."

Chapter 30

THE MASTER'S LIBRARY

Rube gazed in awe. Of all the libraries in the Land that he'd been to, this was by far the grandest. Row upon row of books, all shapes, colours and sizes, filled the walls from floor to ceiling. Long ladders suspended from a rail attached to the ceiling were positioned at intervals around the room. The only natural light was from a single large window at one end of the room, to his left. To his right, a mezzanine floor protruded almost half-way into the room, casting the area below it into gloom. A large table occupied a good area of the floor in the centre of the room, and several books lay scattered on it, two of them open.

He couldn't help himself. Rube walked over to the open books and peered at them. What would the Master (he presumed it was the Master) be reading? He gasped. It was the account of the night of the Visions in Yawbridge. He read:

It began with an image of the gates of Yawbridge. The beautiful tall gates, shut tight. Then they swung open and a baby crawled out. Next thing, the baby became a girl, and the girl grew into an enormous giantess. She grew so tall that she towered over the Land, and even dwarfed the Golden City. Then she turned towards the city gates, stepped over the city of Yawbridge, towards the Chasm, and in a single motion, kicked down the Wall!

He remembered it like it was yesterday. He'd woken up, eager to tell Isabella about his dream. But before he'd had a chance, she'd blurted out her own vivid dream ... and it had been exactly the same as his! They'd soon found out that everybody in Yawbridge had had the same dream. Incredible.

He tapped his finger absently on the page, lost in the memories. It was prophetic: a girl born in Yawbridge would destroy the Wall, impossible as that might seem. It was the talk of the town, and it was not without some excitement that those women who were pregnant wondered whether it would be their child that might achieve this unlikely feat. It soon became apparent that the Master was not so keen on the fulfilment of this dream, as the disappearances began.

There were suddenly a lot more Guards in Yawbridge. New rules were made about women having to go to special centres to give birth, instead of delivering at home with the midwife as was usual. Most women weren't too happy about that, and a group of midwives went to the council to complain. They were never seen again. So, the pregnant women complied, and went to the centres to give birth ... but all the girl babies were taken away from them. Word got around, and some women tried to give birth in secret, but there were huge rewards for people to turn in those baby girls. And they did. Neighbour turned on neighbour, just for some money. Midwives involved in assisting secret births disappeared. Even some pregnant women disappeared. It was an awful time. It went on for two years. Every single girl baby was taken and killed. And then Isabella had fallen pregnant.

For the first three months, they'd been able to hide the pregnancy. Then, they'd gone to visit her sister in Varton. It had taken a month to travel there. They'd stayed a month, then Rube had had to return to Yawbridge. That was the last time he'd seen his beautiful Isabella. Eventually he'd received word from his sister-in-law that the by-then heavily pregnant Isabella had fled for her life after someone dobbed her in to the Guards. But no one had known where she'd gone or what had happened to their baby. Until a month ago, when Freya had told him her real mother was from Yaw. He'd had to wait until he finally tracked Freya's family down in the Golden City to confirm his suspicions, but he'd found out that at the last minute Isabella had indeed fled to Nob, where she'd given birth to Freya on Thomas and Martha's floor. Whilst Thomas was busy washing new-born Freya in the bedroom, a Guard had burst into the house, dragged Isabella off and thrown her to her death in the Chasm. Tears welled up. He blinked them away.

He turned his attention to the other open book. He jumped and the blood drained from his face. It was a register of births and deaths in Yawbridge. And the page was open at the death of a woman called Isabella. Wife of Rube! They were onto him. No time to waste then.

He studied the room once more and spotted what he was after. He made his way towards a bank of cabinets with multiple small drawers, tucked away under the mezzanine floor.

A gas lantern with a clear glass shade hung from the ceiling. It shed enough light so as not to trip over, but not enough to read anything. He fiddled with the small valve and turned the flame up brighter. That was better. Now, what to search for first? He walked along the cabinets until he came to one with the letter 'I' on it. He opened the drawer and flicked through the index cards.

"ID … IF … IM," he muttered under his breath. Nope, not there. He opened the drawer below it. "Aha. IN. Injection, where are you … Aah." He pulled the card out and checked the reference code. He worked his way back along the shelves, inspecting the combination of letters and numbers until he found the one that matched his card. He slid a ladder to the required position and climbed a few rungs. He pulled the first book out with the matching reference code. He climbed carefully back down the ladder and opened the book on the table.

It was some sort of medical book, with diagrams of tubes coming out of one person and leading to another. The title of the diagram was *blood transfusion*. Rube pulled a face and flicked through the book. There was nothing about the injections for the Golden City gates.

He climbed back up the ladder, replaced that book and selected the next one. He climbed down the ladder and opened the book on the table. He scanned the index, but again, whilst there were numerous references to injections and needles, there was nothing specifically about the gates. He climbed back up the ladder, put that one back and pulled a third one out. This time he stayed standing on the ladder whilst he scanned the contents and index. Shaking his head in frustration, he slotted that one back, too, and made his way back to the filing cabinets and slid the card back in place and shut the drawer.

He rubbed his sore hip while he thought. Perhaps 'Golden City'? He located the 'G' drawer and found the relevant index card. When he located the correct shelves, he inadvertently groaned out loud. There was a whole section of shelves, from ceiling to floor. He took a deep breath. Oh well, better start then.

~

Several hours later, he'd lost count of the number of books he'd searched but found nothing. His stomach growled loudly. He clapped his hand to it, in a vain attempt to quieten it. He glanced out the window and was surprised to see it was dark. He was going to have to stay the night here.

Carefully placing the book back on the shelf, he went to the door and listened intently before opening it and slipping out into the hallway. It was deathly quiet. He walked back down the hallway to the awful painting at the top of the landing and back down the marble staircase.

He paused in the grand entrance to listen again, before continuing back the way he'd come: back through the drawing room with the billiard and card tables, back through the dining room with the long mahogany table and large mirrors, and finally down the corridor that led to the servants' quarters and the kitchen.

At the second door he stopped. He heard the murmur of voices. Winston and Peggy. He crept slowly now, careful not to make the floorboards creak. As he passed a closed doorway, light seeping from under it, the voices receded. Good. They weren't in the kitchen then. He stealthily made his way to the kitchen and peered around the door jamb. The fire burned low in the hearth. Apart from a cat curled up on a mat on the hearth, it was deserted. He walked over to the table and peeked under a cloth that was draped over some lumpy shapes. Mmm, fresh bread. One had a flat end, where some had already been sliced off. He glanced around and spotted the bread knife. He cut himself a thick slice and placed the loaf back under the cloth.

Taking a bite, he studied the room. There was a door next to the one he'd come in. He headed over to it. It opened into a small, cold storeroom. Perfect. He helped himself to some cheese, a small salami and an apple. He slipped back out into the kitchen and shut the door behind him. He was about to leave, when he caught a whiff of stew. Unable to control himself, he walked quickly over to the stove. He lifted the heavy lid. Sure enough, there was some stew left over. Salivating at the aroma, he searched around for a spoon. Locating one, he helped himself to a portion. Oh my, that was good. He took another mouthful.

Suddenly, something touched his leg. He got such a fright that he dropped the spoon. It clattered on the floor. It was just the cat! He quickly scooped up the spoon, replaced the pot lid and hurried back to the door. And stopped short.

Winston was standing in the doorway, peering suspiciously into the room. "Who's there?" he called. He heard a noise and stepped into the room. He walked around the table and exclaimed, "Oh, it's you." He bent down and scratched the cat behind its ears. "What are you eating?" he murmured.

Rube didn't wait to see what else Winston might discover. He was already hurrying back along the hallway to spend the night in the library.

Chapter 31

THE DISPLAY

After Alex had left, they had several hours to kill before dusk. They puzzled over the verses but did not come up with any new ideas about what the 'display' or the 'cloud' could be.

"Let's explore," Willow suggested, leaping up from the rock they were sitting on.

"Why not?" Freya carefully wrapped the tablet and secured it in her satchel. She hurried after Willow, who had set off towards the waterfall.

Hopping from boulder to boulder, they passed the crevice where they'd discovered the bees. Before long, tiny droplets of spray from the thundering waterfall misted the air, settling on their faces and clothes. Freya stuck her tongue out and licked her lips. Tyrelian water tasted so good.

Leaping onto a boulder next to Willow, Freya yelled, "Does all water in Tyrelia taste like this?"

Willow glanced at her with raised eyebrows. "You sure do ask strange questions. But now that I think about it, no, it doesn't. For starters, the ocean water tastes *revolting*." Willow screwed up her mouth as though she had some in there at that moment.

"What's *ocean water*?" Freya asked, innocently.

Willow gaped at her. "Are you serious?" Then seeing no hint of guile in Freya's eyes she snapped her mouth shut. "You don't have any oceans in Medar?"

Freya shook her head.

"Okay, so at the edge of Tyrelia, way to the south of here, we don't have a Chasm. We have an ocean. It's a massive expanse of water, but it's salty water." Willow explained. "I swallowed some by accident once. It was horrible." She inadvertently screwed up her face again. "And then there's other rivers with fresh water, and wells with water from the ground. But the best water is definitely what flows out of these Majestic Mountains."

"Well, it's more delicious than any water I've ever tasted before," Freya confirmed.

They reached the cliff that the waterfall was tumbling down. The rocky face was covered in tiny, bright green ferns and mosses, thriving in the damp environment, their roots digging deep into crevices and fissures. Willow walked carefully over the uneven stones right up to the cliff. "Oh, beautiful plants," she exclaimed, spreading her arms wide and hugging the cliff, her head resting on the springy foliage, her eyes shut.

Freya shook her head. "You're strange," she giggled, "but fun." She stepped up beside her to hug the cliff too. "It's not as comfortable as it looks," Freya commented after a moment.

Willow's eyes popped open to respond, but instead she gasped.

"What is it?"

"Look!" Willow pointed at the waterfall. *Behind* the waterfall. "You can climb right behind it."

Standing in front of the waterfall, you would never see it. But positioned as they were with their faces flat against the cliff, they saw that the waterfall arced out from the top of the cliff high overhead, leaving a gap behind it. The cavity swirled with a misty haze. And just visible through the mist was a ledge.

"Wanna try?" Willow's face was all grin.

"You go first," Freya said, thinking about the suspension bridge.

Keeping her belly flat against the cliff and her arms spread-eagled, Willow shuffled towards the curtain of water. She stretched her hand out and thrust it into the mist. Then she shuffled forward so that she was inches from it. She glanced back at Freya, winked, then slithered behind the watery curtain.

Freya strained her eye, but it was so dim that it was not long before she lost sight of Willow. She waited. What was taking so long? "Willow?" she called. No response. She tried again, louder. "Willow? Are you all right?" Still no response.

Freya took a deep breath and, mimicking Willow's movements, flattened herself against the cliff and shuffled behind the curtain of water into the swirling mist.

Just as she entered the watery gloom, something grabbed her hand and pulled. Freya screamed.

Willow burst out laughing. "You should've seen your face," she crowed.

Freya yanked her hand out of Willow's grip and shoved her, blinking back tears. Suddenly, she wished Saff and Thyst were there. "Stop doing that. You could've killed me!" she shouted, her face flushed.

Out of nowhere, she heard Saff call her name. No, it was impossible. Her stone was crushed. She was imagining things.

Willow stumbled backwards. "Hey, hey, I was only playing around. Sorry, I didn't realise you'd get such a fright." She stuck out her hand. "Friends?"

Freya stared briefly at Willow's outstretched hand, before grabbing it and shaking it half-heartedly. "Sure, friends," she sighed. "Come on, let's go back before we miss dusk."

~

Saff was trying to contact Freya. Deep within the Chasm, seated on the broken bridge with Thyst at his side, he focused his thoughts on her. A glowing blue haze swirled around the stone lying on his palm. Briefly, the shapes took on Freya's form.

"Stop doing that. You could've killed me!" The words drifted out of the haze before the shapes melted back into meaningless swirls.

"Freya!" Saff's voice was urgent.

Silence.

"That was Freya," Thyst cried. "She's in trouble. We have to get to her."

~

Freya and Willow sat on a boulder side-by-side, gazing up at the sky. The sun sank gradually lower and lower towards the horizon.

"Look!" Willow pointed. A tinge of faintest pink coloured the sky.

"See any clouds?" Freya asked, swivelling her head all around.

"Nope."

Freya's head froze mid-swivel. "What's that sound?"

"What sound?"

"Shh. Listen."

A faint flapping sound grew steadily louder and louder.

"Look!" said Freya.

Willow's gaze followed where Freya was pointing, across the

other side of the ravine.

They leapt to their feet, staring.

From an invisible crevice, hundreds and hundreds of bats flapped out into the canyon. They formed a swirling mass, swooping and spiralling about the cliff, feasting on the tiny insects. More and more of them issued from their cave, thousands upon thousands. The flapping of their wings filled the air.

Freya slapped her hands to her mouth, gazing in awe at the black swarm, circling up into the sky like a giant tornado, forming fantastic shapes in the now dusky purple heavens. A giant cloud of bats. What a display!

Chapter 32

THE BOOK

Rube awoke with a start. He gazed up at the unfamiliar ceiling, trying to work out where he was. Then he heard the noise again. The one that had woken him. Suddenly, it all came flooding back. He was in the Master's library! He immediately turned himself invisible and crawled on his hands and knees over to the balustrade of the mezzanine floor. He peered down between two bulbous timber supports.

An old woman was bustling about below him, flicking her bright blue feather duster over the table. She was wearing a black uniform with a white apron and white mob cap. It wasn't Peggy from the kitchen. She was whistling tunelessly. That was what had woken him.

She finished dusting the table and turned her attention to the book shelves. She started on the one immediately to the left of the door and climbed the long ladder. She dusted the top shelf. Stepped down a rung. Dusted the next shelf. Stepped down a rung ... Bother, this was going to take a while. Rube crawled back to the corner where he'd spent the night and leant his head back against the book shelf behind him and closed his eyes.

There was a book with some studs in its spine digging into his neck. He moved his head, but they were still there. Annoyed, he turned around to inspect the culprit. He suppressed a gasp. It was *A History of Tyrelia*. He'd slept right next to it all night—it had literally been under his nose … or rather, above his nose.

Slowly, he slid it out and dragged it closer to the balustrade where it was a bit lighter. He daren't adjust the lighting whilst the old woman was still in the room. Talking of which, where was she? He hadn't heard the doors opening and closing.

A creak on the stairs coming up to the mezzanine gave him the fraction of a second's warning that he needed to turn the book invisible. The blue feather duster heralded the presence of its owner whose head appeared a second later. She continued her tuneless whistling as she worked her way around the bookcase at this upper level.

Rube gathered the book and backed up to the balustrade. He held his breath as she came within half a metre of him. Suddenly, his eyes started watering and his nose tickled as the disturbed dust wafted around his face. He grabbed his nose and squeezed it tight, willing himself not to sneeze. Blood rushed to his face and he felt like he was about to explode. *Hurry up!*

Suddenly, she dropped her duster. "Deary me," she said, breathing heavily as she bent down to pick it up.

Rube took the opportunity to exhale and take another breath. He sidled along the balustrade, distancing himself from the woman.

Several more minutes passed while she finished her task. At last, with a final flick of the duster, she headed towards the stairs. As she stepped on to them, Rube took a big step away from her. But his injured hip prevented his intended movement. He lost his balance and fell heavily onto his hands and knees. He only just managed to keep the book from spilling out of his grasp. The woman froze, her duster poised mid-air. She slowly turned around to gaze at the mezzanine. "Hello? Is somebody there?" Her eyes darted around.

Rube stayed where he was. He daren't move.

A sudden gust of wind rattled the window. "Oh," the woman exclaimed. "Silly me. It's just the wind." She spun back around and continued down the stairs.

Rube slid forward until he was lying on the ground, then rolled on to his back. Gripping the book with one arm, he flopped his other over his eyes. That had been too close.

Another half hour passed before the woman finally finished her dusting and left the library. Only when he heard the doors close did Rube sit up and crawl over to the balustrade to confirm that she was indeed gone. Gripping the book, he descended to the main floor and sat down at the far end of the table, nearest the window. He placed the book on the table in front of him and stared at it.

It was a very large book, almost as long as his arm, and as thick as the width of his hand. It was a wonder he hadn't dropped it when he fell. He absentmindedly rubbed his knee. He had fallen rather heavily on it.

The book was bound in a deep red leather cover. An embossed leafy vine motif wound its way around the edges. The title was etched in gold leaf in the centre: A HISTORY OF TYRELIA. He took a deep breath, then reverently opened the cover.

A colourful map took up the inside cover and first page. He studied it eagerly. They had been right about Tyrelia surrounding Medar: the latter was represented as a grey oval roughly in the middle of the map. Tyrelia spread around it in vibrant shades of greens, blues and browns. A row of white-tipped mountains marched along the top and a deep blue ocean ran along the bottom. He found where Freya had entered Tyrelia. It was near a town called Beta. He wondered where she was. Whether she was all right.

It suddenly struck him how very far away she was. His daughter. With renewed determination, ignoring his throbbing knee, he turned the page. Ah, the table of contents. He scanned the long list. Where to start? Should he start at the beginning? If not there, where? The problem was, he didn't really know what he was looking for. Just that he was certain that this book held the secret he needed.

He'd start at the beginning then. He turned the page and read:

Chapter One – The Ancient

Nobody really knows where the Ancient came from or what he looks like. The earliest memories of Tyrelians is that he simply is. He dwells in the Majestic Mountains. The Ancient has great power and only desires good for all people. Thus, Tyrelia is an abundant land of plenty that is there for all who choose it.

But those who do choose to live there shall abide by the Four Laws of Tyrelia:

1. *Honour the Ancient*
2. *Put others first*
3. *Use your gifts for good*
4. *Follow the Rules*

Rube nodded as he recalled Freya telling them about the Laws.

The Laws are there to protect all and provide peace. However, the Ancient also allows free will. Thus, some people choose not to follow the Laws, or even choose not to dwell in Tyrelia. This greatly saddens the Ancient. He mourns for those who turn their backs on him and Tyrelia. His tears form the Helix River, and as such the waters of the Helix River are imbued with the power of the Ancient himself.

It is said that many people have been healed of vile afflictions just by drinking a drop of water from the source of the Helix River. This power is the greatest power known in all the Land.

Rube stared at the last sentence: *the greatest power.* Could it be? His heart started beating faster. Was it possible, that the power of the waters from the source of the Helix River could break the power of the injection? The more he thought about it, the more certain he became that he was right.

He desperately wanted to read further, but he also desperately wanted to leave the Master's house. He made a snap decision. This book was too precious to be hidden away here in the Master's library. He picked it up, and, holding it close to his chest, made his way out of the library

.

Chapter 33

THROUGH THE RIFT

After the spectacular display of the cloud of bats, Freya and Willow returned to spend the night with Alex and his flock of sheep.

Early the next morning, after a quick breakfast of bread and cheese washed down with water, they set off to locate the bat cave. As they emerged from the trees once more, Alex scanned the opposite cliff face eagerly.

"Where is it?" he asked.

Freya and Willow both pointed to roughly the same section of cliff, about one hundred metres from the waterfall, but halfway up the face.

"I can't see it," Alex complained.

"Yeah, you wouldn't know it was there, without seeing the bats come out," Freya said.

"Oh, Alex. You should've been here. It was *amazing*." Willow exclaimed. "C'mon, you've gotta see this passage behind the waterfall." She clambered off over the boulders.

Alex and Freya followed suit, leaping from rock to rock.

Alex was slightly taller than Willow, and more muscular. He

passed his twin and beat her to the waterfall.

"After what you told me you did to Freya, there's no way I'm letting you go first," he laughed, and disappeared behind the curtain of water.

Willow flashed a grin at Freya, who had caught up, and was right behind her. She shrugged. "Fair enough. Do you want to go first, Freya?" she asked, sheepishly.

Freya nodded. "Thanks." She slipped past Willow and stepped through the swirling spray on to the ledge.

She waited a moment for her eye to adjust to the gloom, before shuffling forward.

Alex stood halfway along, his back pressed to the cliff, staring at the water cascading past him and plunging into the river a hundred metres below.

He glanced at Freya approaching, before turning back to stare at the waterfall. "It's beautiful," he murmured.

Freya similarly flattened herself against the cliff beside him and gazed at the silvery sheet of water. An ever-changing pattern of light and dark played within the curtain. If she stared at it for a while, it even looked like the water was flowing upwards in places. It was mesmerising.

Willow joined them and also stared at the water. After a while she sighed. "Hey," she called, "I think we should keep moving."

"Yes, of course," Alex said. He shuffled along the ledge until he emerged, blinking, into the sunlight on the other side of the waterfall.

"That was cool," Freya said as she stepped out, wiping her face with her sleeve.

"Yes, and wet." Willow stepped out behind her, also drying her face. She whipped her cap off her head and flapped it around, spraying droplets of water everywhere.

"Right. Now where?" Alex asked, looking at the girls.

Freya shaded her eyes and stared up at the cliff face. "It looks a bit different from this angle," she said, frowning. "Anyhow, it's further down that way." She set off.

As on the other side of the canyon, there was a narrow strip of flattish land, strewn with a tumble of big boulders. They clambered from one to the next. The cliff face near the waterfall was green with lush ferns and mosses. But as they moved beyond the fine mist, the growth morphed into small bushes, clinging to the cliff for dear life, concealing the rocks underneath.

Every few minutes, Freya and Willow stopped and checked out the cliff face towering above them, conferring as to whether they were there yet. The fifth time, however, was different.

"What do you think? Isn't that the big bush we were talking about? The one with the white flowers?" Freya asked.

Willow turned to gaze across to the opposite bank where they'd stood the previous night to obtain their bearings, trying to memorise the correct location. "Yes, I think so. Look, there's that weird lumpy boulder." She pointed.

"Right, so now all we need to do is climb." Freya walked over to the cliff and pushed her way past the scratchy bushes. She placed her foot on one of the trunks where it protruded from the bank, stretched overhead and grabbed two more branches, and heaved herself up.

"Are they strong enough to hold your weight?" Willow asked anxiously.

Freya bounced a little bit. The trunk held. "Seems to be," she called. She pulled herself up and wedged her other foot onto a trunk a little bit higher.

CRACK!

The bush gave way and Freya slid the short distance back down the cliff face. Rubbing her scratched arms, she stepped back from the cliff face. "Actually, I don't think that's going to work," she announced.

"You think?" Willow raised her eyebrows, a smirk playing at the corner of her mouth. She reached over and plucked a twig out of Freya's braid.

"Hey, come and look over here," Alex shouted. He had been exploring further along the bank.

"Where are you?" Willow called.

He stepped out of the bushes, beckoning them, his face flushed. "I think I've found a way up."

Freya and Willow ran to him.

Alex pulled the nearest bush back and stepped aside. "Look."

Freya walked around him and stopped.

"What is it?" Willow craned her neck to look over Freya's head. "Oh. By the Ancient! A path."

Concealed behind the shrubbery, it was incredible that Alex had even spotted it. But there it was: a narrow flight of steps carved into the cliff.

Freya hugged Alex. "You're the best," she exclaimed, heading up the path.

Alex's face turned a deep red.

Willow punched him on the arm. "Good job, bro," she said. "What's red?" She winked as she swept past him to follow Freya up the path.

Alex let the bush snap back into place and hurried after the girls.

Up, up, up they climbed, higher and higher, all the while completely hidden by the shrubs and bushes clinging to the rocky cliff.

The path cut back on itself once, twice, before abruptly ending at the entrance to the rift. Even standing right in front of it, you couldn't see it due to the rock formation jutting out parallel to the cliff like a wall. Freya slipped behind it and stopped, blinking in the sudden dimness.

It stank.

Willow rounded the rock wall behind her and bumped into her, knocking her forward.

"Ugh!" Freya exclaimed.

"I agree," Willow said. "What a smell. Phew!"

"I wasn't talking about the smell … although, yes, that's bad enough. But what am I standing in?" Freya asked, pointing at the ground.

Alex stepped into the space, holding his nose. "That," he said in a nasal voice, "is guano. Bat poo." He grinned.

"Oh," Freya said, pulling a face. Then she craned her neck to look above her. "I see."

There, suspended upside down from the ceiling of the rift, were hundreds of thousands of bats.

"How cool," breathed Alex.

At the sound of their voices, some of the creatures shuffled and squeaked, but most of them remained serenely hanging from their perches.

Now that their eyes had adjusted, Freya realised that the cave was not completely pitch black. Light entered the space from somewhere else, quite a distance away.

Trailing a hand along one wall, Freya carefully stepped deeper into the cavity. The guano squished and squelched underfoot.

"This is totally revolting," Willow announced cheerfully.

"I agree," Alex said in the same cheerful tone of voice.

Freya glanced back at them. "It's official," she said. "You're both completely weird."

"Thanks," Willow said. "What a compliment."

Freya shook her head in exasperation and inched her way deeper into the crevice.

The passage bore hard left. Off in the distance she discerned a lighter shade of grey. More by feel than by sight, they worked their way towards the patch. As they got closer, Freya felt the passageway twisting once more. She rounded a bend and found herself facing a solid wall, but with a narrow slit letting in sunlight, high above her head.

"Be careful, it's the end of the tunnel," she shouted to the others.

She was joined by Willow and Alex. They all gazed up at the narrow hole. Freya felt the wall below it with both hands, trying to find hand or foot holds. Nothing.

"I don't think we can climb this," she said.

"Here, let me try." Alex stepped forward and carefully felt the surface. Willow joined in.

"You're right," Alex conceded after several minutes. "Hang on, stand back, I'm going to try and jump."

Willow and Freya obediently moved to one side. Alex took a few steps back then, crouching slightly, sprinted forward and leapt up to the opening, his arms outstretched above him. *Smack.* His hands slapped the cave wall, well below their intended target. He slid to the floor of the cave in a heap.

"Are you all right, Alex?" Willow asked, rushing to her brother's side.

"Yuck. Yes, apart from being covered in guano." Alex pushed himself up again and wiped his hands copiously on his trousers. "Well, that's not going to work," he declared.

Willow snorted. "You're a genius. So glad you explained that for us." The mirth was clear to hear in her voice.

"Oh, shut up," Alex said crossly.

"Do you think I can climb up on your back, Alex?" Freya asked.

"Sure." Alex stood sideways against the wall and crouched so that his back formed a platform.

Willow helped Freya up. Freya steadied herself against the wall and stretched as high as she could. "I can't quite reach," she announced, disappointed.

"I reckon you will if you stand on his shoulders, though," Willow said, excited.

"Okay, let's give that a go." Freya grabbed Willow's outstretched hand and jumped off Alex's back. *Squelch.*

Suddenly, Freya started spitting.

"What are you doing?" Willow demanded.

"Some guano splattered into my mouth when I landed," Freya moaned.

"Yuck!"

"All right. When you're ready, Freya," Alex said.

Freya wiped her mouth with her sleeve. "Okay, ready. How are we going to do this?"

"Start with a piggy back," Alex instructed, "then I'll bend over a bit, and you climb up my back and get your knees onto my shoulders. Brace yourself against the wall. When you're balanced, tell me and I'll slowly straighten up. Oh, and you'd better give your shield to Willow."

She did as directed. "Okay, you can straighten up now," she called.

Slowly, slowly, Alex stood up.

"Be careful," said Willow, standing with her arms out in case

Freya fell.

"I've got it," grunted Freya. She gripped the base of the opening, then manoeuvred herself off her knees to a standing position on Alex's shoulders. The opening was now at chest height. She wedged her elbows onto the ledge and then, with an enormous effort, pulled herself up into the opening. "Wow!" she exclaimed in awe.

"What is it?" Willow and Alex asked in unison.

Freya tore her gaze away and peered back down at their upturned faces. "There's another whole valley here," she said, breathlessly.

Chapter 34

ESCAPE FROM LEVEL SEVEN

Clasping the book to his chest, Rube tiptoed down the long hallway, back to the landing at the top of the wide sweeping stairway down to the grand entrance. He paused momentarily. With a sore left hip and throbbing right knee, he'd better take care down these stairs. He switched the book to his right arm and gripped the marble balustrade tightly with his left hand. He contemplated making himself visible so he could see where he was stepping but decided against it. Too risky.

Placing each foot carefully, he slowly made his way down the staircase. Stepping off the final tread onto the black-and-white checked marble floor, he paused to catch his breath and adjust the book back under his other arm. Maybe it hadn't been such a good idea taking the book?

He was just about to head towards the drawing room when he heard a clatter and voices outside the main door. Two Guards swung the doors open inwards and snapped to attention either side, their eyes staring straight ahead. Rube stood rooted to the spot. What should he do?

He heard horses stamping and gravel crunching under the

hurrying feet of servants. It didn't sound like anyone was coming inside just yet. Rube took a tentative step towards the open doorway, his gaze flicking between the rigid Guards and the opening between them. No reaction. He took another step. So far so good. A third step. He picked up his pace slightly. Now he was directly between them. He held his breath as he walked past them. Then he froze.

Now that he was outside, he saw that the Master had dismounted his carriage and was ascending the stairs, heading straight towards him! Rube scuttled to the left and stood at the edge of the tread, willing the Master to stride straight past him.

The Master was clothed completely in black: a swirling black robe with a hooded cowl hung low over his face, concealing it in shadow. He wore black leather gloves and boots and carried a black walking stick. He strode purposefully up the stairs but paused on the top tread. The one Rube was standing on. He turned his head slowly this way and that, sniffing. Then stopped, staring straight through him.

The hair on the back of Rube's neck prickled. Beads of sweat broke out on his forehead and trickled down his face. He barely dared breathe.

Then the Master snapped his head back towards the house and swept inside. The Guards closed the doors smartly behind him.

Rube sank down and sat on the step, shaking. The Guards were standing right beside him, but he didn't trust himself to move just yet. He mopped his brow and forced himself to breathe slowly. Gradually, his heart calmed.

A servant had been standing by the horses, patting their noses. Now he tugged at the reins and they stepped forward. The wheels of the carriage crunched on the gravel.

With a start, Rube realised that this was his chance to escape: the noise would mask the sound of his own footsteps. He pushed himself to his feet and descended the short flight of stairs to the gravel driveway. The horses and carriage were continuing past the palace, but Rube turned to the left. He scurried across the driveway and stepped gratefully on to the manicured grass. Then he hurried back parallel to the drawing and dining rooms, towards the kitchen where he'd come in the day before.

He slowed to a walk once more. Unlike the previous day, there was no heavy fog. He admired the exterior of the palace as he went. The entire building was a dirty mustard colour—well, what could be seen of it. Most of it was covered in ivy, all the way up to the roof, three stories above him. Large windows were framed by solid white surrounds with wide sills. From this angle, he couldn't see the glittering gold roof he'd spotted on his way in.

Up ahead was the kitchen. Part of the well jutted out from behind the building. Keeping to the grass on the far side of the courtyard, he emerged from behind the house. Ah, there was the path he'd come in on.

Suddenly, two dogs started barking. He almost dropped the book in fright. They were chained up in a kennel right beside the back door. But they were straining towards him. The back door burst open and Winston came running out. "Max! Buster! What is it?" He stared wildly around, trying to locate the source of his dogs' distress.

Rube hurried off as fast as he could, limping heavily now.

Winston went to his dogs and tried to calm them down. But they would not.

Then Rube heard some words that caused dread to stab through him.

"Okay, okay," Winston muttered. He fumbled at their collars and unclipped their chains. "Go find that ghost."

The dogs bounded away to the spot where Rube had been. They sniffed around, whining, their noses to the ground, then with a howl, streaked off towards Rube.

Disregarding his injuries, Rube ran for his life. He had a few minutes' head start, but they were gaining on him rapidly. Shifting the book to his left arm, he fumbled around in his robes. Where was it? With relief, his fingers closed around a hunk of salami he'd been saving for later. He flung it wildly to his right as far as he could.

It materialised in mid-air the second it left his grasp. And it did the trick. The dogs saw the morsel of meat and changed direction towards it. They pounced on it and briefly fought over it, snarling.

Rube reached the gate in the fence and tried to open the latch with one hand. He couldn't do it.

The dogs had made short work of the salami and were once again racing towards him.

Rube shoved the book between two fence railings. Immediately it materialised, lying on the ground outside the fence. Rube fumbled with the latch, panting for breath. The dogs were almost on him. It opened! Rube squeezed through and slammed the gate on the dogs' noses. They barked and whined, jumping up at the gate. Rube scooped up the precious book, dusted off the dirt and hurried off, not looking back. He didn't stop until he'd passed safely back into Level Six.

He really was too old for this.

Chapter 35

THE HIDDEN VALLEY

From her perch in the crevice, Freya gazed in wonder at the secret valley spread before her. To her left, a hundred metres or so away, another waterfall tumbled down the cliff face, plunging into a pool at the bottom. The valley floor, far below her, was lush green except for a flash of silver where a river wound its way from the pool at the base of the waterfall to a fissure in the cliffs at the opposite end of the valley. Apart from that, the valley was completely contained within the mountain.

"Freya," Willow yelled impatiently, "move out of the way so I can climb up there."

"Sorry. Just a minute." Freya scrutinised the cliff face immediately below her. "There's a ledge here!" she exclaimed. She wriggled her way forward, then rolled onto her stomach so that her legs were dangling below her. Slowly, she eased herself down. When her toes found the ledge, she let herself drop on to it. "All right," she called out, "you're good to go."

Willow climbed onto Alex's back and steadied herself against the cave wall. He stood up slowly, and she climbed on to his shoulders. With her extra height, she easily attained the opening and heaved herself up and around. She pulled her legs up and swivelled around to face the valley. She gave a low whistle. "By the Ancient, Alex, this is amazing." She smiled back down at him.

"Yeah, well, I'll have to take your word for it," he grumbled, handing Freya's shield up to her.

Willow's face fell. "Maybe I can pull you up?" she suggested. "Watch out, Freya, I don't want to kick you in the face."

Freya grabbed her shield then moved out of the way of Willow's legs, thrashing about out of the opening above her, as Willow manoeuvred herself around.

Willow draped herself so that her torso was hanging back inside the bat cave, then extended her arms down to her brother. "Can you reach?" she asked.

Alex stretched up on tiptoes. Not close enough.

"Hang on, I'll try and reach further down," Willow called. She shuffled and wriggled around. "Freya, can you hold my legs to stop me from slipping?"

Alex reached out to her once more. Their fingertips brushed. "I could try jumping, but you'd need to catch my hands, then pull me up," he suggested doubtfully.

"Worth a shot," Willow said.

Alex crouched down, then leapt up. Willow caught his hand for a moment, then his fingers slipped from her grasp.

"Try again," Willow urged.

Once more, he crouched, then leapt.

"I've got you," Willow crowed. She tried pulling him up, but the angle was too awkward, and she didn't have the strength. "Arrgh," she grunted.

Alex let himself drop once more to the cave floor. "Looks like I'm staying put," he said, his voice heavy with disappointment.

"I'm sorry, Alex."

"That's all right. I have to get back to the sheep, anyhow," he said, turning away.

Willow turned and said something to Freya, then pushed herself upright so she was once more sitting in the opening. "Hey, Alex!" she called out.

He turned back to his sister. "Yeah?"

"Thanks. We couldn't have done it without you. You know that, right?"

He nodded.

"And we'll see you soon, a few days tops, I suppose."

"Sure. Bye, Freya!" his voice drifted back to her.

"Bye Alex," Freya called. "Thank you for everything."

As Alex turned and made his way back the way they'd come, Willow watched him until he was out of sight. Then she sighed and twisted herself back around to face the valley. Her face brightened. "Oh well, just us again," she said.

Freya nodded.

Willow rolled onto her stomach and eased herself down until she was standing on the ledge beside Freya. "Right. Now what?" she asked, expectantly.

"Well, I reckon we head towards that waterfall," Freya said. "Mainly because the path doesn't go anywhere else," she added with a grin.

Willow nodded. "Excellent idea. After you."

The path was wide enough for one person, but they were high up, and Freya didn't fancy falling. Unlike in the other valley, this cliff face was mostly devoid of vegetation, consisting only of crumbling rock.

The path descended gradually. It did not take long before a fine mist danced in the air currents and the roar of the waterfall drowned out all other sounds.

Freya rounded a bend in the track and stopped.

Willow came up behind her. "What is it?"

There, adjacent to the waterfall, was a cave entrance. Freya glanced at Willow, biting her lip. Her heart beat faster.

"Go on," Willow urged.

Freya walked up to the cave entrance and peered in. She couldn't make out much in the relative dimness. "Hello?" she called. "Is anyone there?"

Silence.

"Hello?" she called again.

This time she heard a noise. A cough.

From the depths of the cave, she discerned a figure shuffling towards her. It was an old man, bent with age, leaning on a staff. He was completely bald and wore robes, not too dissimilar to those the Watchers had worn. He shuffled right up to her and peered closely at her.

"Er," Freya mumbled, disconcerted by his stare, "are you the hermit?"

He blinked solemnly at her with watery grey eyes under bushy eyebrows. He stared at her deformed eye, then his gaze flicked to Willow standing behind her. He bobbed his head, and a smile tugged at the corner of his mouth. "Yes, Freya, I am."

Freya and Willow gaped at him.

"How do you know my name?" Freya demanded breathlessly.

The old man chuckled but ended up in a coughing spasm. When he'd recovered, he tapped the side of his nose with a bony finger of his free hand. "Heh, I know more than just your name, young lady," he said. He beckoned as he turned away. "Come along now, you have much to learn. You too, Willow."

Willow shot a startled look at Freya, who just shrugged and pulled a face. There was nothing for it but to follow the old man into the cave.

Chapter 36

THE HERMIT

Willow paused as she stepped into the cave. "So," she said, waving her hand towards the wall at her left. "You're an artist, are you?"

The old man bobbed his head. "Mmm, yes, of sorts," he said.

Freya turned to look at the wall Willow had indicated. A small patch near the entrance to the cave showed the beginnings of a painting: a human outline, surrounded by a bit of blue and green. She hadn't noticed it as she walked past.

"Come, come," the old man said, shuffling forward. "We have much to discuss. Come, sit." He indicated some well-worn chairs constructed of branches twined together and padded with cushions stuffed with grass. Woven mats covered the floor of the cave.

Freya shrugged the shield off her back.

"Can I see that, my child?"

"Yes, of course." Freya held it out for the hermit to inspect. "Sorry, it's a bit sticky," she mumbled, wiping her fingers on her tunic.

With bright eyes, he brushed his fingertips lightly over the studded surface. He studied the stone in the centre intently. "Well, well," he murmured.

"Do you know where it came from?" Freya asked eagerly.

"Maybe. Maybe. But we'll talk about that later. Sit, now."

They sat as bidden. The hermit eased himself into his chair with a sigh. Leaning towards Freya, his hands resting on his staff, he studied her for a moment before clearing his throat. "Freya, my child, why have you come?"

Freya's mouth dropped open. "Well, of course, it's because …" She stopped. Why *had* she come? She'd been so intent on following the clues that the tablet revealed, that she'd forgotten the original reason for her journey. So many strange things had happened since entering Tyrelia that she had more questions than ever. Why had the shield appeared on her back? Why were Tyrelians radiant, and why was it starting to happen to her? Why were the vibrations so strong for her? How had they travelled two hundred rata within the vibrations? Was her purpose to obtain answers to these questions? Her mind whirled.

She thought back to when she'd first come here. Why had she passed through the Wall in the first place? Was it to find Tyrelia? Well, she'd done that the minute she'd crossed the Chasm, all those weeks ago. Was it to find out how the Watchers might pass through the Wall? She'd thought the Ancient would be able to tell her how to do that. So, was it to find the Ancient? Suddenly, she knew. "I'm hoping that you can tell me where I can find the Ancient, so I can free my family from the Golden City," she said breathlessly. "Unless …" a thought occurred to her. "Are you the Ancient?" she asked timidly.

The old man chuckled and shook his head. "No, my child, I'm not. Although I *am* very old."

The disappointment was visible in Freya's face. "I guess my tablet did say 'the hermit'," she mumbled. "Oh. That reminds me. My tablet said that you were to give me a task."

"Hmm. Yes," the hermit bobbed his head.

"And a gift," Willow exclaimed. "Don't forget about the gift, Freya."

"Can I see your tablet, Freya?"

"Yes. Of course." She felt around inside her satchel, which she had set on the floor beside her, and extracted it. She unwrapped the object and passed it to the hermit.

He took it reverently in both hands. He ran a hand over the smooth, glassy surface, pausing at the numbers etched at the bottom. He turned it over. "I have only read about this. It's an honour to hold it. Tell me, child, what words has it revealed to you?"

"Here or in Medar?"

"Both, if you please."

"Sure. So, in Medar these are the words I got:"

Freya recited:

Tyrelia! Land of gold
A land so lovely to behold
O, land of beauty, land of light
Joyous refuge, pure delight

Tyrelia! That land so fair
Of meadows green and clean pure air
Of stately trees in forests vast
Of ancient rocks from ages past

Majestic mountains, white with snow
Their crystal tears to rivers flow
Splashing sparkles dance up high
Painting rainbows in the sky

Swathes of splendid floral hues
The land with colour do imbue
The golden sun smiles down from high
As he marches 'cross the sky

As flaming sunset turns to night
Stars and moon cast silver light
On all who choose to live lives free
From the Master's tyranny

He has no claim to any throne
He long ago was overthrown
By the Ancient, true and just
In whom all living things can trust

Who alone has claim to rule
Tyrelia, beyond the Wall
Tyrelia! O, land of gold
O, land so lovely to behold …"

Willow sighed. "Oh Freya, that's lovely!"
Freya smiled. "I know. And now, the words that appeared in

Tyrelia. It starts the same as before, but needed different substances to make the words appear."

Tyrelia! Land of gold
A land so lovely to behold
O, land of beauty, land of light
Joyous refuge, pure delight

Tyrelia! That land so fair
Of meadows green and clean pure air
Of stately trees in forests vast
Of ancient rocks from ages past

Fresh clean air, sparkling waters
Quench your thirst, sons and daughters
Head to the place with sulphurous steam
To free Medar from the Master's schemes

Go up Helix River, to its source
At the waterfall—a powerful force—
Follow the sounds of birds up high
Of honey bees buzzing as they fly

When sunlight fades to shades of grey
At dusk watch for nature's display
From whence the cloud comes, will reveal
The path which is elsewise concealed

Deep within the mountain rift
Find the hermit to claim your gift
He will guide you in your task
You won't receive if you don't ask."

Freya's voice died away. The hermit's eyes were shut. Had he fallen asleep?

He stirred and opened his eyes. "Thank you, child. Hmm. Yes." He handed the tablet back to Freya. "You'd better keep that safe. Who knows, perhaps more words will appear in due course."

Freya took it and wrapped it back in its leather covering before tucking it carefully back into her satchel.

"So, Freya." The hermit coughed.

Freya looked at him expectantly.

"I think you already know what your task is."

Freya blinked. "Oh. To free my family from the Golden City? Is that it?"

"Not quite. The tablet already told you. *To free Medar from the Master's schemes,*" he quoted.

"But … how?"

"The Ancient will guide you."

"Oh! So, you *do* know where I can find him. Can you take me to him?" Freya's voice was full of hope.

The hermit shook his head gently. "Yes and no. I can't take you to him. But I can teach you how to hear his voice—how to listen to his instructions. Do you want to learn?" He raised his bushy eyebrows at her.

Freya didn't even hesitate. "Oh, yes," she exclaimed. "I would love that."

The old man smiled at her enthusiasm. He wagged a bony finger at her. "It's not an easy thing, my child," he warned. "There is a choice to be made. And much to be studied."

"What do you mean *a choice*?" Willow demanded.

The hermit glanced at Willow, before fixing his gaze once more on Freya. "You will need to choose to become a citizen of

Tyrelia. To follow the rules of Tyrelia. To follow the Ancient's rules."

"Oh, that's not so hard," Willow scoffed.

The hermit raised his eyebrows at Willow. "Isn't it?" he asked. "Even rules about allowing only one person on a bridge at a time?"

Willow blushed a deep red. "That was only a bit of fun," she muttered.

"Willow," the hermit said gently, "the Rules aren't there to stop you having fun. They're there to give you freedom."

Willow's head snapped up, a look of confusion in her eyes. "Huh? How does that work?"

"When everyone follows that Rule, they know that they are free to safely cross the bridge at any time, without any fear of harm."

Willow nodded slowly. "Oh. So, the Rules are there for my own good? Huh. I always sort of figured that they were there to ruin my fun."

Freya shook her head at Willow and rolled her eyes. She turned back to the hermit. "I think *I* can follow the Rules, though. So, my answer is yes. I do want to become a citizen of Tyrelia. What do I need to do?"

"First, you need to swear an oath. Then you will need to drink a cup of water from the source of the Helix River."

"Oh. That's all?"

"Yes. But I must warn you, there may be some side-effects from drinking the water."

"Side-effects? Like what?"

"Everyone's different. Because you're not from here, I'm not entirely sure how you will react."

Willow interjected. "When I did it, I only felt a bit woozy for a few minutes, then I was back to normal." She smiled encouragingly.

"What? Wait a minute. You've done this?" Freya asked, incredulous.

Willow shrugged. "Yeah. Everyone does the ceremony when they turn twelve. It's like a rite of passage."

"Oh." Freya was quiet while she processed this piece of information. "Well, if everyone's done it, I suppose there's no reason for me not to do it."

"Good, good," the hermit bobbed his head. Leaning heavily on his staff, he pushed himself to his feet. "Both stand up too," he said, motioning with his hand.

They stood.

The hermit cleared his throat. He stared intently at Freya. "Repeat after me, Freya: "I, Freya, daughter of ... what are your parents' names?"

"Oh," Freya said, flustered. "My real parents or my adoptive parents?"

A look of surprise flitted across the hermit's face. "All of them, I suppose."

"All right. So, my ma and da who raised me are Martha and Thomas. But my birth father is Rube and my birth mother ... I don't know her name!" she said, panicked.

The hermit laid a reassuring hand on her shoulder. "It's okay. So: *I Freya, daughter of Martha, Thomas, Rube and his wife ...*"

"I Freya, daughter of Martha, Thomas, Rube and his wife ..."

"... promise to honour the Ancient ..."

"... promise to honour the Ancient ..." Freya repeated.

"... Put others first ..."

"... Put others first ..."

"... Use my gifts for good ..."

"… Use my gifts for good …" Freya's eyes widened as she said this one.

"… and follow the Rules of Tyrelia, for as long as I shall live."

"… and follow the Rules of Tyrelia, for as long as I shall live."

The hermit nodded at her.

Freya breathed a sigh of relief.

"Wait here one moment. I'll just go fetch the water." He shuffled off through an archway to another cave that Freya hadn't noticed earlier.

He was not gone long before he re-emerged, carefully carrying a wooden cup. "Here it is," he said. "Drink, drink."

Freya took the cup and, raising it to her lips, drank it in big gulps. "Aah," she said, when she'd finished. "That was good."

Suddenly she staggered. Dropping the cup, she fell forward on to her hands and knees. Her vision blurred and her head felt like it was stuffed with cotton. "Oh, I don't feel well," she moaned. She lay down on the mats on the cave floor.

Willow dropped to her knees beside her.

Freya's eyes rolled back into her head and her face went very pale.

As if from afar, Freya heard Willow gasp. "Freya, Freya! Are you okay?" She fanned her hand over Freya's face. She felt Freya's wrist for a pulse. "There's no pulse!" she cried. She leapt to her feet and confronted the old man. "What have you done to her?" she demanded, tears leaking out of the corners of her eyes.

The hermit backed away, shaking his head, looking down at Freya with wide eyes.

"Nothing, nothing," he mumbled. "This has never happened before. I swear it, by the Ancient!"

Willow turned and fell back to her knees beside Freya. "Freya," she whispered, "please don't be dead."

Chapter 37

RUBE RETURNS

Jack and Martha sat at the table eating dinner. Well, Jack was eating. Martha was pushing the potatoes, peas and sausages around her plate. They weren't talking. There was nothing to say. They both jumped when someone knocked on their door.

"I'll get it, Ma," Jack said. His chair scraped on the flagstones as he jumped up. He peered out the window before opening the door.

It was Leena. She was beaming from ear to ear. "Hello Jack. Martha, would you and Jack like to pop over after dinner for a cup of tea?" Her words tumbled out.

Martha stared at her. "Are you all right? You look flushed."

Leena nodded vigorously. "Yes, yes, quite well. I think you should come as soon as you can."

Jack turned to look at his mother, his eyebrows raised.

Martha nodded wearily. "Sure, Leena, we'll come over shortly."

"Make sure you do." Leena waved cheerily and hurried off.

Jack shut the door behind her. "Do you think Hank's printed another poster?"

Martha shrugged. "Could be. You'd better finish your dinner, Jack. Then we can go and find out."

Five minutes later, they were knocking on their neighbour's door. It opened immediately. "Come in, come in," Leena said. She glanced quickly around at the empty street outside before closing the door. "Go through to the living room and make yourselves comfortable," she instructed them.

Hank and Sam were already there, with the same grin on their faces that Leena had had. Before he could ask what they were all so excited about, Rube materialised seated on the couch.

"Oh," Jack exclaimed. "Rube, you're back early. You've only been gone five days."

Martha went over to Rube and sat down next to him, placing her hand on his shoulder, her eyes full of concern. "Oh Rube, you look terrible. What happened?"

Jack scowled. It was just like his mother to fuss about someone when, clearly, she was the one who needed to be fussed over.

Rube rubbed his knee. "My dear lady, it's been quite an adventure. I've been up to the Master's palace. Ah. There's Leena with the tea."

Amidst their exclamations of surprise, Leena walked in carrying a tray with their drinks and some cake and served them all before sitting down herself.

Sam piped up, his mouth full of cake. "Rube, did you see the Master?" he asked, his eyes huge.

Rube chuckled. "Well, young man, as a matter of fact I did."

Everyone gasped.

"But let me start from when I left here."

~

When Rube had finished recounting his tale, Sam asked the

question they were all thinking: "Can we see the book?"

"Yes, of course. If you don't mind, young man, can you bring it to me? It's in the spare room, on the bed."

Sam jumped up and trotted off to the bedroom to fetch the book as instructed. He came back walking slowly, clutching it awkwardly to his chest, his eyes peering over the top.

"Set it down here, lad." Hank patted the low table.

Everyone leaned forward as Rube took the book from Sam and laid it reverently on the table.

"Oh," Martha sighed, "it's beautiful."

Jack was the only one who didn't look impressed. "So, instead of freeing Da, you've risked your life for some old book?" he accused.

Rube looked up at Jack, startled. "Jack," he said gently, "this book holds the key to freeing *everybody*."

"What do you mean?" Hank asked, wrinkling his brow.

"I mean," Rube said, colour rising in his cheeks, "I think I've discovered how to break the power of the injection."

"Oh my," Leena exclaimed, her eyes wide. "What is it?"

Rube opened the cover of the book and flicked to the first chapter. He cleared his throat and read out the passage.

"So ..." Leena said, when he'd finished, "... you think that the waters of this Helix River will act as an antidote to the injection?"

Rube nodded. "Yes. That's exactly what I think."

"But you don't know for sure," Jack pointed out.

"No," Rube conceded, "but it's worth trying."

Hank cleared his throat. "Let's assume you're right. That this Helix water breaks the power of the injection. How do you plan on getting it?"

Rube sighed. "That, my friend, is indeed the challenge. I'll need to leave the city and contact the others so we can make a plan."

"What about Da?" Jack demanded. "Are you going to free him?"

Rube furrowed his brow. "Hmm. Yes, I suppose I could try."

"When? Tomorrow?"

Rube rubbed a weary hand over his face. "I need to contact the others first. That's most important. After that I could try."

"But ..." Jack started.

Leena interrupted him. "Jack," she said gently, "Rube's very tired. He's had a hard week. Let's all get a good night's sleep. He needs to recover before he can help your father properly."

Jack scowled.

Martha, who had been sitting quietly beside Rube, patted his hand. "Yes, you get better, Rube, so you can help us all." She smiled wearily at him. She stood up and reached out a hand to Jack. "Come on son, time to go home. Thank you, Leena, for a lovely cup of tea. Goodnight everyone."

Jack stood up. "Yeah. Goodnight."

~

Jack tossed and turned. He couldn't sleep. *Maybe* Rube would try to free Da. But only after he left the city again tomorrow morning. And hadn't he said something about it being too dangerous for him to be seen around here? What if he decided to get as far away as possible? Then who knew whether his da would ever be released?

And why was it so urgent to tell the others about the Helix water? It wasn't like they would be able to do anything about it for ages. Even if they miraculously managed to ask Freya to collect the water tomorrow, it would take her months to travel back here. It would take the Watchers even longer from the Cave

People. The water probably wouldn't even work. Besides, living in the Golden City wasn't that bad. It was better than Nob. Even if they got the stupid water, he wouldn't drink it. It was a waste of time.

He sat up, threw off the covers and quickly got dressed. Quietly, he sneaked through their kitchen and let himself out the front door.

Chapter 38

A HIDING PLACE

Martha and Jack had just left. "That's one angry young man," Rube commented to Hank and Leena.

Leena wrinkled her brow. "I'm so worried about them. First, they lost Freya, now Thomas. Rube, is there anything you can do?"

Rube sighed, rubbing his hip. "I suppose I could go and see if I can find out where Thomas is."

Hank spoke up. "But first, we need to hide that book. The Guards may have our house under watch. They could come in and search us at any time. We can't risk keeping it here."

"Do you have someone else you can trust with it?" Rube asked.

"No, I don't, but I have an idea." Hank stood up. "I know you're tired, Rube, but I'll need your invisibility for this." He picked up the book. "Are you ready?"

Rube nodded and placed his hand on Hank's shoulder. "The question is, are *you* ready, Hank?" And with that, he turned them both invisible.

Hank took a tentative step forward. And another. Then he

ruffled Sam's hair.

Sam had been sitting on the couch, quietly listening to the adults making their plans, savouring this opportunity to stay up a bit later than usual. But when his father touched him unexpectedly, he yelped and leapt from the couch.

Hank burst out laughing.

Rube made them both visible again. "Hank," he reprimanded sternly, "now is not the time for pranks. Come, let's go."

Hank looked sheepish. "Sorry, Rube." He pulled an apologetic face at his son. "Right, let's do it."

Once more, Rube turned them both invisible. They walked to the back door and opened it a crack. Rube sensed Hank peering out, before slipping outside. They walked along the back of the house, around the side then paused before setting off down the street.

They walked for about fifteen minutes, taking a right here and a left there, but always heading downhill, towards the Level One wall.

Hank stopped outside an industrial-looking building. He fumbled in his pocket. Rube heard a faint clanking sound, followed by a scraping noise. Then the small timber door swung open in front of them. They stepped inside. Only once Hank had closed the door behind them, did Rube allow them to both become visible again.

The smell of fresh parchment and ink assailed his nostrils. They were inside the Level One printing press.

Hank stuffed his keys back into his pocket. "Follow me," he whispered. He headed deeper into the dark building, between the shadowy shapes of two massive printing presses. Rube hurried to keep up with him.

At the back of the room, Hank unlocked another door. They

entered the room and Hank closed the door behind them. "Stay there, Rube, I'm going to find a candle. Here, hold this." He thrust the book into Rube's hands.

Rube waited patiently for what seemed an age, but was in reality less than a minute, whilst Hank fumbled around somewhere off to his right.

Suddenly, the light of a small flame pierced the darkness. Rube blinked, allowing his eyes to adjust. Hank tipped the candle to a second one, and a third. That was better. They could see now.

"So, I found this hidey-hole when I first got promoted to press manager and got this office. Set the book down there, Rube." Hank gestured to the desk with the three candles on it. He walked over to a filing cabinet that was almost as tall as himself, with four drawers in its face. He slipped his fingers between it and the wall and slid them carefully down, about halfway. "Here it is."

Something clicked and the whole cabinet swung outwards. There in the wall, was a door.

"Where does it go?" Rube asked, his eyes big.

"Oh, nowhere, but wait till you see it."

Hank loosened the iron ring that was set into the door and twisted it. There was a scraping sound, and the door swung inwards. He stepped backwards as the smell of cold, musty air filled the room.

They peered into the opening. It was pitch black.

Hank hurried over to the desk and grabbed a candle. He held it out to Rube. "Here. Take a look."

Rube thrust the candle into the opening. He sucked in his breath. A short flight of stairs led down to what appeared to be a reasonably large cavern. He nodded. "This will be perfect,

Hank. Can I go in?"

"Sure. I'll grab the book."

Rube edged down the stairs. Once in the cavern, he could only just stand up. His white hair brushed the rough roof. He slowly spun around, holding his candle up as high as he could. A low bench was hewn into the four walls. Rube promptly sat down.

Meanwhile, Hank had come down the stairs with the book.

"I reckon you could fit twenty people in here," Rube exclaimed. "What do you think it was used for?"

Hank hunkered down on his haunches and scratched his beard. "I dunno. But I'm guessing maybe to hide whisky from the Guards?"

Rube snorted. "You're probably right," he agreed. "Well, I guess we stash the book over there." He bent down and felt the ground. "It feels dry enough—although I wish we'd brought something to wrap it in."

"Oh, I think I can rustle something up." Hank ran back up the stairs. After a moment, he reappeared with a stack of paper. "Here, we can use this."

They wrapped some around the book, until it looked like a parcel. Then stacked some on the floor for good measure and placed the wrapped book on top of the stack.

Rube brushed his hands together. "Good," he said, satisfied. He smiled at Hank. "Let's go."

Hank nodded and climbed back up the stairs, Rube behind him. He carefully shut the door and closed the cabinet back over it. Hank opened the door back into the printing warehouse a crack before snuffing out the candles. After waiting a moment for their eyes to readjust to the darkness, they crept back out between the presses. Rube turned them invisible before they slipped back outside.

Just as they made it back to Hank's house, they heard a noise. They froze. They stared with surprise as Jack slipped out his front door and headed off down the street in the opposite direction.

When he was out of earshot, Hank whispered, "Where do you suppose he's going?"

"I don't know," Rube replied in hushed tones, "but I intend to find out. You'd better go home, Hank. See you later." He squeezed Hank's shoulder, then hurried off after Jack.

Chapter 39

TRANSFORMATION

Freya moaned.

Willow's head jerked up. "Freya! You're alive!" She laid her hand on Freya's forehead. "Are you okay? How do you feel?"

The hermit, who had been sitting in his chair, staring intently at Freya, stirred, and leaned forward.

Freya opened her eyes and blinked at Willow. "I feel … different," she said dreamily.

The hermit cleared his throat. "Heh, yes, yes." He said, his head bobbing. "It's the transformation. Only the waters from the source of the Helix River can do that."

Freya eased herself up into a sitting position. "Transformation?" she asked. She raised her hand to her deformed face and felt the scars around her eye. "Nothing's changed though," she said dejectedly.

The hermit shook his head. "No, no, my child. It's changed you on the inside! You see, for the Ancient, it's not your external appearance that's important. It's the condition of your heart. Look." He pointed at her chest. "See for yourself."

Freya looked down at her chest and frowned. "What do you

mean?" she asked.

Willow had been staring at Freya. "I know what he means," she said gently. She took Freya's arm and pushed her sleeve right up. "Look."

Freya gasped. Her skin was as radiant as Willow's now, with light playing under the surface.

Willow cleared her throat. "Freya, there's something else."

Freya swivelled her head towards Willow. "What? There's more?"

Willow nodded and stretched out a hand towards Freya's head. She formed a fist and knocked gently on her skull. A dull metallic sound echoed around the cave.

Freya's hands flew to her head. She felt the thing that was on it. It was cold and solid. Metal. She was wearing a helmet. "Why did you put this on me?" She demanded, frowning first at Willow then at the hermit.

The hermit shook his head, a look of wonder on his face. "It just appeared as you lay there. One moment it was just you; the next it was there. Just like the shield. I believe it's part of your gift."

"Oh," she breathed. She turned to the hermit. "Thank you." She smiled.

He shook his head. "No, no. Don't thank me. Nothing to do with me. Neither the helmet nor the transformation. That occurred from the power within the waters of the Helix River."

Freya frowned. "But I don't understand. How could there be power in the water?"

"Well, the Helix River is formed by the tears of the Ancient himself, you know. Always flowing."

Freya's eyes went wide. "Why would the Ancient be crying?"

The hermit smiled a sad smile. "He mourns for all the people who don't believe in him. For all the people in Medar who have never been told about him, such that they have no hope of ever believing in him and coming to Tyrelia."

Freya looked indignant. "Well, that's silly. Why don't the people in Tyrelia just go to Medar and tell them all about the Ancient? About Tyrelia?"

The hermit sighed. "Yes. You would think they would. But they don't. Most people think it's up to the Adelphi to do that. But the order of the Adelphi has all but disappeared here."

Freya recalled Saff telling her about the Adelphi—the order of Tyrelians established to protect the secret of the talking stones whilst they were trapped in Medar. She knew that only five stones remained in Medar—no, four now that hers was destroyed!—but Saff had told her that most of the Tyrelians had managed to escape before the Master raised the Wall. She had assumed that Tyrelia would be full of Adelphi using their stones and powers of invisibility.

"Why?" she demanded.

"That, my child, is a long story," the hermit replied.

Willow and Freya glanced at each other.

"I don't think we've got any other pressing business," Willow said dryly.

"Well then," the hermit said. "Are you hungry? I can tell you while we're eating."

"Sure," they chorused.

Chapter 40

BETRAYAL

Rube hurried to keep up with Jack, but at the same time was careful not to make a noise. This limited his movements to a fast walk, which was all he could manage with his painful hip and knee.

Jack disappeared around a corner up ahead. By the time Rube reached the corner, there was no trace of Jack. No, wait, there he was, rounding the following corner. He was hard to make out, sticking to the shadows like that. He'd better not lose him. But as Rube rounded the next corner himself, he saw he needn't have worried. They had arrived at the Guard house next to the main city gates, and Jack was knocking on the door. What could he be up to? Rube walked quietly towards Jack.

The door opened and a Guard poked his head out. Quiet words were exchanged. The Guard opened the door wider to admit Jack inside.

Rube hurried forward, his heart hammering in his chest.

Just as Jack walked past the Guard, another voice called from deeper within the building. The Guard holding the door open paused to respond to his colleague. This gave Rube the fraction of a second that he needed to slip inside behind Jack.

He pressed himself against the wall as the Guard closed the door then strode off down the corridor, beckoning Jack to follow him.

They stepped into a room where two other Guards were biding their time during their midnight shift. Rube loitered outside in the corridor such that he could see into the room.

"Who's there, Krupp?"

"Well, Gorm, this here pup's got some urgent news for us." Krupp jerked his thumb over his shoulder at Jack.

"I know where the traitor Rube is," Jack blurted. "The one you're offering ten thousand for."

Gorm chuckled. "And where would that be?"

Jack cleared his throat. "I'll tell you, but only if you show me that my da's all right, first."

The Guards raised their eyebrows at each other. Krupp spun on his heel. "Follow me," he barked at Jack. He grabbed a flaming torch off the wall sconce. He marched out of the room and down the corridor, deeper into the building. Rube followed at a distance.

At the end of the corridor, they took a left, then down a flight of stairs. "Hey, wake up!" Krupp yelled.

Another Guard, who'd been snoozing on a stool at the base of the stairs leapt to his feet with a yelp.

"Take me to that Thomas prisoner," he commanded.

The sleepy Guard fumbled at the keys hanging on the ring at his belt as he stumbled off down the corridor.

The solid brick walls were now punctuated on both sides with doors featuring vertical iron bars.

They stopped at the fifth door on their right. The prison Guard rapped on the iron bars with a short truncheon. Someone moaned. "Hey Thomas! Wakey wakey. There's someone here to see you."

Jack rushed to the bars and, grabbing them in both hands, peered into the dark cell. "Da! Da! It's me, Jack!" he called.

The person in the cell moaned again.

Jack spun back to the Guards. "I can't see him. I can't tell if he's okay," he accused, eyes flashing.

"Calm down, pup," the prison Guard grumbled. He singled out a key from his keyring and inserted it into the lock. It screeched as he turned it, then stopped, stuck. "By the Master!" He swore in frustration. He twisted the key roughly and the mechanism clicked. He thrust the door open with his shoulder and stumbled into the cell. "Pass me that torch," he ordered over his shoulder. He grabbed it and waved it in front of him.

A bedraggled figure huddled against the far wall. The cell stank. The prison Guard walked over to him and shook his shoulder. "Thomas. Your son is here."

Jack had followed the Guard into the cell. "Da! It's me, Jack. Are you all right?"

Thomas rolled over, shielding his eyes with his arm.

Jack rushed to him, pushing the Guard out of the way. "Da," he said gently.

Thomas squinted at him. "Jack?" he croaked.

Tears leaked out of the corner of Jack's eyes. He blinked rapidly and brushed them roughly away with the heel of his hand. "Yes, Da, it's me." He carefully slipped his arm under Thomas's shoulders and eased him upright.

"So, as you can see, he's alive," Krupp said. "Now you show us where that traitor is."

"No," Jack flung over his shoulder, "you let my father go, then I'll show you."

Krupp chuckled. "You drive a hard bargain, pup. Tell you what, you show us where that traitor is, and we'll let your father go."

Jack gazed at his father, his lips pressed into a tight line, his hand on Thomas's shoulder. "Can you at least give him something to eat and drink?"

Krupp nodded curtly at the prison Guard, who promptly left. He returned a few minutes later with a jug and a hunk of bread.

Jack grabbed the jug and pressed it to Thomas's lips. "Here, Da, drink this."

Thomas took a sip then, placing his hands on top of his son's, he raised the jug higher to take a big swig. Sighing, he wiped a trickle of red liquid off his chin. Wine.

"And some bread." Jack tore off a hunk and pressed it into Thomas's hand.

Thomas chewed rapidly, resting his head against the wall. He washed it down with another gulp of wine. "Thanks, son," he said.

"All right, let's go now," Krupp barked.

Reluctantly, Jack stood up. "I'll see you soon, Da." He followed Krupp out of the cell and the jailor locked it behind them.

As Krupp and Jack disappeared around the corner, the prison Guard, who had just sat back down on his stool, suddenly slid gracefully to the floor, unconscious. A faint clinking of keys was followed by the familiar screech of the lock. Thomas's cell door swung open once more.

Thomas peered into the dimness. "Who's there?"

"Shhh." Rube materialised in front of him.

Thomas's eyes became saucers. "Rube! How did you get here?"

"I followed Jack," Rube whispered. "I've come to free you. We don't have much time. Let me help you up." Placing his hands under Thomas's armpits, he heaved him upright. "Can you walk?"

Thomas stood a moment, leaning against the wall. "I'll have to lean on you." He placed his arm around Rube's shoulders and they walked slowly out of the cell.

Rube pulled the door shut behind them. They shuffled down the corridor, then whilst Thomas leaned against the wall, Rube slipped the keyring back onto the unconscious Guard's belt. "Right, I'm going to turn us both invisible now, but you'll need to be as quiet as a mouse."

Thomas nodded.

It was a slow journey back home. Thomas was very weak, and they had to rest often. Suddenly, they heard voices. They froze and pressed themselves flat against the closest house.

Three Guards appeared around the corner. "What a waste of time that was," one complained.

"Still," Krupp replied, "now we know where he's hiding out, it'll just be a matter of time before we catch him. As long as we've got his father, I think that pup'll be quite amenable to informing us where that Transient is."

The other two Guards chuckled, as they walked right past the invisible Rube and Thomas. When the Guards were well out of earshot, Rube let out a breath. He shook his head. "I must admit, I hadn't thought this through. I hadn't actually planned on freeing you right now, you see. I just happened to see Jack sneaking off down the street and ... well, you know the rest. Of course, neither of us can stay at yours or Hank's, now."

"What are we going to do?"

"Well, as it happens, I know just the place we can hide." Rube grinned. "Come on. Not too much further, my friend."

They made their way to the rear of Hank's house. Thomas sank gratefully onto the steps, while Rube slipped back around the side of the house and tapped cautiously on a window. Immediately, the curtain twitched aside and Leena's face peered out. Rube allowed himself to briefly become visible. Leena's mouth formed an 'O', then quickly snapped shut. The curtains closed and, within seconds, the back door swung open.

As soon as Leena's eyes fell on Thomas sitting there, she sprang into fussing mode. "Thomas! You look awful. Come in. Let me make you a nice cup of tea. Have you eaten?"

Rube helped Thomas upright. "Hush. We can't stay." He bustled them inside and shut the door.

Hank walked into the kitchen, tucking his shirt into his trousers. "No, you can't. Did you know that the Guards have just been here, searching for you?"

Rube nodded, grimacing. "I gathered. Lucky we got rid of that book."

"I know." Hank swiped a hand through his curls.

Leena made them a cup of tea and then packed a basket full of food. Hank gathered together some blankets. They spoke only in whispers. In less than fifteen minutes, Hank, Rube and Thomas were ready to leave again.

Hank supported Thomas with one arm, his other full of blankets. Rube stood behind them and placed his hand on Hank's shoulder. "Ready?"

Hank nodded once. "Let's go."

Rube turned the group invisible as they slipped out into the darkness.

"Be careful," Leena whispered to the empty room, wringing her hands.

Chapter 41

REUNITED

Early the next morning, Leena knocked on Martha's door. Jack opened it. He had dark rings under his eyes. She craned her neck, trying to see around Jack, careful to keep her voice neutral. "Is Martha there?"

Jack stepped aside. "Sure, come on in."

Martha looked up as her friend approached her. She, too, had dark rings under her eyes. "Hello Leena, what brings you here so early?"

Leena pursed her lips and stared at Jack for a second, before pulling out a chair and abruptly sitting down. "Did Jack tell you what he got up to last night?" she blurted out.

Jack turned bright red and hung his head.

Martha stared from one to the other. "No. What did you get up to, Jack?" she asked in measured tones.

"I tried to secure Da's release," he mumbled. "I saw him, Ma! He looks awful. We have to get him out of that prison." He snapped his head up defiantly, his eyes flashing.

Martha sucked in her breath. "What happened?"

"He brought Guards around to our house in the middle of the

night, is what happened," said Leena.

"Rube! What's happened to Rube?"

Leena cut her eyes at Jack. "Luckily, he wasn't there. We don't know where he is." She grabbed one of Martha's hands and squeezed it. "Pop around after the Games, won't you? Alone." She glared at Jack.

Jack pushed himself up from the table. "I'm leaving anyhow. I have to go to the Games." He stormed out of the house.

"You can't trust him, Martha," Leena said quickly. She grasped her friend's hands. "But Rube and Thomas are safe."

Martha's eyes went big and a flush crept up her neck.

Leena smiled and nodded, "Quickly. I'll take you to them now before the Games start. But we won't be able to stay long — we should still serve at the ale tent, so as not to arouse any suspicions." Leena gave Martha a big hug. "Do *not* let Jack know," she warned into her ear.

Martha cleared away the breakfast things, grabbed her basket and followed Leena next door.

A Guard watched them from across the road.

Once inside, Martha clasped Leena's hands. "Where is he, Leena? Is he okay?" she asked breathlessly.

Leena smiled and nodded. "We've hidden both Thomas and Rube in a secret room at Hank's printing press. He's weak, but he'll be all right. Are you ready?"

Martha nodded.

They left via the front door, chattering gaily as they went, as though they didn't have a care in the world.

By now the street was filling up with people heading off to the Games. They joined the throng. The Guard yawned.

When they arrived at the printing press, Leena didn't even knock, but just opened the door and went straight in. The place was deserted. They went directly to the rear, and Leena rapped smartly on Hank's office door.

"Enter. Oh, hello love."

Leena bustled in and Martha followed.

Hank casually walked towards a filing cabinet against the back wall.

Martha clapped her hand to her mouth as he fiddled with something at the back of the cabinet, and the whole thing swung into the room, revealing a door behind it.

Hank tapped out a sequence of five quick knocks, before opening the door. He handed Martha a candle. "Down you go."

Martha and Leena made their way carefully down the stairs. A candle had been lit below, and they focused on the glow. Hank shut the door behind them.

As soon as Martha reached the bottom of the flight of stairs, she handed the candle to Leena, then flew into Thomas's arms. "Thomas, Thomas, my love. How are you?"

Thomas wrapped his arms around his wife and rested his head on hers. "I'm better now that you're here," he said gruffly.

Leena skirted around the couple and gave the basket to Rube. "Here you go. You must be starving. And how are you feeling?"

Rube smacked his lips. "Why, thank you kindly, Leena. I'm sure it will be delicious. And we've both slept well last night, so feeling much better, thank you." He whipped off the checked cloth and fished out a cold chicken drumstick. He bit into it hungrily.

Leena laughed. "I see you were hungry! Make sure you leave some for the others … Talking of which—" she cut her eyes to Martha and Thomas, whose arms were still wrapped around each other. "I might just take some of this up to Hank."

Rube quickly swallowed his mouthful. "Hrmph. Yes, I think

I'll follow you up."

Five quick knocks on the door at the top of the stairs and they were back in Hank's office.

"It was getting a bit … hot down there," Leena explained in response to Hank's raised eyebrows. "I might just wait here with you for a bit, if you don't mind."

Rube helped himself to a bread roll out of the basket. "And I need to leave the city. Shouldn't be too hard with everyone distracted by the Games."

Rube saw himself out of the building. He would've liked to have taken the book, but he didn't trust his hip and knee yet to support the weight of it. He set off down the street and out of the city. At last. It was hard to believe it had only been six days since he had last been outside the walls. It felt like much longer.

He paused outside the Level One gate and gazed up. Sure enough, there was a word there. He'd never noticed it before. It read I N V I D I A. He must remember to see if the book explained those words.

He strolled alongside the moat towards the small copse of trees, eyeing the sky. Plenty of time until sunset. He settled down to wait.

~

Rube fished out his talking stone. Holding it flat on his palm, he concentrated his thoughts on Saff. A red glow emanated from the stone, growing and swirling, darker shades mingled with lighter hues, until they clearly resembled Saff.

"Rube!" Saff exclaimed. "It's so good to see you. Did you find what you were looking for? Are you all right?"

Rube didn't waste words on pleasantries but cut straight to the chase. "I found it, Saff. I got all the way to the top—Level Seven—and found a book about Tyrelia in the Master's library.

I think I know what the antidote is for freeing people from the Golden City."

Saff's jaw dropped open and he glanced to his right. Thyst must be sitting next to him. "What is it?"

"It's water from the River Helix. In Tyrelia."

"Water from the Helix River in Tyrelia?" Saff sounded unsure.

"That's what I said," Rube confirmed with a nod.

"But ... but," Saff spluttered. "How are we supposed to get that? Just march into Tyrelia and divert the whole river into Medar?" He snorted.

"Of course not!" Rube replied. "I don't know. I haven't figured it out yet."

Saff raised his eyebrows. "Well, in that case, we'd better start rebuilding that bridge. Won't be entering Tyrelia otherwise. And I'd better start believing in the Ancient."

"Yes, you had. I'll be relying on you both to find Freya."

Chapter 42

ADELPHI

"On the day that the Master smashed the southern bridge, all the Adelphi in Medar fled to the remaining three bridges," the hermit began.

"Wait," Freya interrupted. "Three bridges? There are two more bridges? Where?"

The hermit peered at her from under his bushy brows. "Oh dear, you have a lot to learn. Let me find a map." He pushed himself out of his chair, groaning as he did so.

"I'll help." Willow leapt to her feet.

"Follow me." He shuffled off to the rear of the cave. Shelves filled a section of cave wall from floor to ceiling. They were partitioned off at intervals to form a multitude of cubbyholes, each compartment holding several scrolls. "Light that candle over there and pass it to me, please," he said, gesturing towards a table further back, covered in scrolls and parchment.

Willow did as she was bidden.

Leaning his staff up against the wall and gripping the shelves instead, the hermit held the candle up to the cubbyholes, ensuring the flame did not threaten the scrolls but was close enough to read the labels on each. He hummed and hawed, inspecting first one label, then another. After a few moments, he exclaimed, "Aha!" and passed the candle to Willow. He extricated a scroll and gave that to Willow too. Then he grabbed his staff and hobbled back to his chair, leaving Willow to snuff the candle and hurry after him.

Freya helped him to sit down again and Willow handed him the scroll. He undid a black ribbon and spread the scroll out on the low table, from which Freya had cleared the food. She gazed at it eagerly.

The hermit circled his finger over the oval roughly in the centre of the map. "That's Medar. There's the southern bridge, which the Master destroyed, with the Alpha gate." He pointed to the one Freya had discovered at the home of the Cave People.

"There's the one I came into Tyrelia on," Freya said excitedly, pointing to the north of Medar.

The hermit nodded. "Yes, the northern bridge and Beta gate." He pointed to the right of the oval, near the Shady Desert. "The eastern bridge with the Zeta gate and," finally he pointed almost directly at Nob, "the western bridge and Gamma gate."

Freya gasped. "Nob! There's a bridge next to Nob."

The hermit bobbed his head. "Yes, yes."

"But nobody knows about it. How could we have not known?"

The hermit fixed her with his piercing gaze. "If you would stop chattering, I can explain it to you."

Freya felt her face redden. "Sorry," she mumbled.

The hermit cleared his throat. "As I was saying, when the Master destroyed the Alpha bridge, fifteen of the remaining twenty Adelphi escaped via the other three bridges. They made their way back to Adelpha and had a great meeting, known as the conclave. The meeting lasted three days. By the end of the conclave, they had a plan: they would wait a month before even attempting another crossing. Then, they would go in pairs at monthly intervals, trying a different gate each time. And so, they did."

Freya couldn't help interrupting. "But what about the Wall?"

"What about the Wall?"

"How did the Adelphi pass through it?"

"Oh. Well, the Adelphi never stopped believing," the hermit explained, matter-of-fact.

Freya frowned. "I don't understand."

The hermit circled his hand above Medar on the map. "Why, my child, it's a Wall of Unbelief. As long as one believes in the Ancient and, more importantly, believes that he's more powerful than the Master—then the Wall does not exist."

Understanding dawned on Freya. "That explains a lot."

The hermit continued his story. "In addition to visiting Medar, every day they would try to contact the Adelphi trapped there. But they must've gone into hiding, and they could not contact them. This went on for a whole year. The Adelphi who ventured in to Medar came back with stories of close calls, due to the Land crawling with Guards and the people of Medar so fearful that they would not talk to them. They even started coming back with stories about how the Master had become more powerful than before. Bah!" The hermit thumped his staff on the ground.

Willow jumped.

The hermit frowned even more fiercely, his eyes all but disappearing under his bushy brows.

"So ... the Master hadn't become more powerful?" Freya ventured eventually.

The hermit looked up, startled, as if he'd forgotten they were there. "No. Of course not. Well, he does have some power. But no more than what he had before. No more than what the Ancient allows him to have." He sank back into a reverie.

They waited in silence for a bit. Willow glanced at Freya, eyebrows raised. She cleared her throat. "Then what happened, Sir?"

The hermit sighed and shook his head. "Then … they stopped going. One by one. The first was Pearl. She fell in love and went off to have a baby. Not that having a baby should stop you being an effective Adelphi," the hermit grumbled. "Next was Peri. He went hunting in the Great Forest one day and was never seen again. Amber and Beryl were sisters. They set up a business in Heneva. And so it went. Everyone got busy doing other things. They forgot their Adelphi vows. They gave up hope of ever freeing those trapped in Medar. The chief Adelphi, Nyx, contacted them all. And, one by one, they came to him and relinquished their stones." The hermit shook his head sadly. "No new apprentices were found to replace them. The stones lie untouched to this day in the vault in Adelpha." His voice died away.

Freya sat in silence for a while when he was done, thinking about the story. "It's not right," she said, at last, her eyes flashing.

Willow shook her head in agreement.

Freya leapt to her feet. "There's got to be someone in Tyrelia who's willing to become an Adelphi."

The hermit nodded. "I think there might be someone." He stared at her intently.

Freya squirmed under his gaze. "Who, me?" she squeaked. "But I'm only fourteen."

He smiled. "And being fourteen stopped you discovering the long-lost path to Tyrelia and finding me, did it?" He raised his eyebrows at her.

Freya blushed. "Well, no. Of course not. But I can't go back to Medar by myself and rescue everyone."

"No, no. That you can't." He fixed his gaze on Willow. "But of course, you needn't be alone."

It was Willow's turn to look uncomfortable. "What are you looking at me for?" she asked. She inclined her head at Freya. "I mean, I want to help her, but how? I don't have any special powers."

He pursed his lips. "No, you don't. Not yet, anyhow."

Freya put her hands on her hips. "What are you suggesting?"

"My children," he beamed at them, "how do you feel about training to become Adelphi?"

Freya and Willow looked at each other, their stunned expressions mirrored in each other's face. Slowly, Freya broke into a smile.

"Yes," she said. "Yes, I would."

"Well, in that case, you'll need this." The hermit picked up Freya's shield. Laying it on his lap, he prodded the clasp covering the stone in the centre. The intricate mesh covering the stone lifted. The hermit tipped the shield up, spilling the stone into his palm. He extended his hand towards Freya, revealing the small, multi-hued oval stone, the size of a quail's egg. It was a talking stone.

Chapter 43

A NEW QUEST

"Freya!" Rube was so surprised to see her face in the red swirls of his talking stone, that he dropped it altogether. A few seconds passed before he re-established their connection. "But, by the Master! Thank the Land you are alive. What happened? Where have you been?"

"Well, it's rather a long story," she replied. "I fell out of a tree and shattered my old stone. But you know my shield? It turned out that there was a talking stone embedded in the middle of it. I only just found out myself." Then, in a wondering tone, "I found him, Father." It felt good calling him that.

He blinked hard. "Who? The Ancient?"

"No, not the Ancient. The hermit. Oh, of course, you don't know about the clues," she exclaimed. "Father, it's been amazing. I met Willow and her twin Alex, and they helped me solve all the new clues that the tablet showed me: the sulphurous steam and the honey and the bats. Then when we finally found the hermit, I became a citizen and now I've got a helmet, too!" The words tumbled out like a dam bursting.

"Freya, Freya, slow down," Rube chuckled, her enthusiasm

contagious. "You'd better start from the beginning."

And so, Freya recounted her adventures to an incredulous Rube, starting with discovering how the tablet had showed new messages at the outskirts of Beta, until she'd arrived at the hermit's cave in the Majestic Mountains.

"You say you drank the waters of the River Helix?" Rube queried.

"Yes. The hermit called what happened to me 'the transformation'. But it only changed me on the inside," she said forlornly, touching her scarred eye with her free hand.

"No, don't be sad. It confirms what I thought." It was Rube's turn to share his adventures and, most importantly, his discovery of the book in the Master's mansion. "So you see," he concluded, "I believe that the Helix River waters contain the power to reverse the effects of the injection. I need you to bring some back to the Golden City immediately."

"No!" Freya exclaimed. "I can't. I need to train to become an Adelphi. Like you."

Rube shook his head. "Freya …"

Freya glanced to her right, then said, "The hermit wants to talk to you … Father."

The image of Freya's face disappeared from Rube's red stone glow and was immediately replaced with that of a bald old man with bushy eyebrows and a hooked nose.

"Greetings, Watcher Rube," the hermit said. "I would have preferred to introduce myself in person, but …" he cleared his throat, "this will have to do. My name is Brother Nyx."

Rube gasped. "B … Brother Nyx? Then … Your Excellency." He bowed his head. "It is an honour to meet you."

Freya shot a glance at Willow. "Excellency? What's going on?" she hissed.

Willow shrugged, pulling a face.

The hermit glanced at Freya. "I'm the head of the Adelphi," he explained, his eyes twinkling. He turned his attention back to the black swirling shape in his palm. "And Freya's right. She does need to train properly before returning to Medar. Willow too. They need to learn how to make themselves invisible. How to tell people about the Ancient. After all, there's no point in rescuing people from the Golden City if they can't pass through the Wall, is there?"

Rube sighed. "You're right, of course. We can wait. After all, we've already waited a thousand years. I suppose we can wait a little bit longer. But, Freya, please don't take *too* long."

Freya stared at the swirling shape of Rube's face on Nyx's palm. "I won't," she promised. "I'll get there as soon as I can."

ACKNOWLEDGEMENTS

Writing a book is really hard. This one has been as much of a learning curve as my first one, Medar. Once again, the time I have spent working on this book is time away from my family. Therefore, to my husband Craig, thank you, thank you, thank you. For your endless support, your ideas and your time being my Alpha reader.

Thanks also to my Beta readers and the Tauranga Writers' Group. You gave me much needed encouragement and some great ideas to improve the story.

Finally, to my editors, Grace Bridges and Chad Dick, thank you for your eagle-eyes and expertise. I have learnt so much from you.

Sharon Manssen
December 2018

ABOUT THE AUTHOR

A professional engineer by training, Sharon is currently a quality, environment and sustainability manager in a large, global engineering consultancy firm. Therefore, writing a novel may seem an unlikely fit. However, Sharon's upbringing involved moving to Belgium when she was 12 and completing her secondary schooling in Flemish, with French and German also taken as subjects. This is where her enjoyment of languages was born.

Upon completing her schooling, she returned to New Zealand, obtained her engineering degree, met her engineer husband, married and commenced working. Their careers took them back and forth between New Zealand and Bangkok over a fifteen-year period, during which time they added two beautiful children to their family (one born in each country). In addition to learning Thai, Sharon also realised she had a story inside her, which she then proceeded to write over the next ten years, squeezing writing in between raising a family and working full time.

OTHER BOOKS BY S R MANSSEN

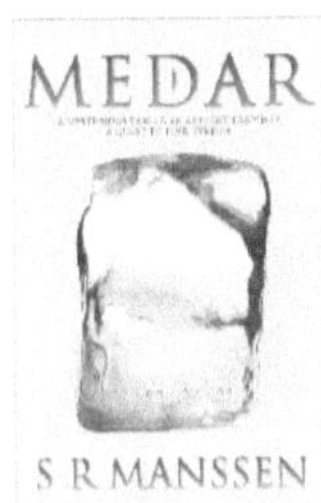

MEDAR
When Freya finds a mysterious tablet telling her about a beautiful land beyond the Wall that is free from the evil Master, she doesn't think anybody will believe her.

CONNECT WITH ME

I hope you enjoyed reading my book as much as I enjoyed writing it. You can follow me on these social media platforms:

Website:
http://www.srmanssen.com

Facebook:
https://www.facebook.com/realmtrilogy/

Smashwords:
https://www.smashwords.com/profile/view/SharonManssen

LinkedIn:
https://www.linkedin.com/in/sharon-manssen/

Email:
realmtrilogy@gmail.com